ABOUT THE AUTHOR

Simone Buchholz was born in Hanau in 1972. At university, she studied philosophy and literature, worked as a waitress and a columnist, and trained to be a journalist at the prestigious Henri-Nannen-School in Hamburg. In 2016, Simone Buchholz was awarded the Crime Cologne Award and was runner-up in the German Crime Fiction Prize for *Blue Night*, which was number one on the KrimiZEIT Best of Crime List for months. The next in the Chastity Riley series, *Beton Rouge*, won the Radio Bremen Crime Fiction Award and Best Economic Crime Novel 2017. In 2019, *Mexico Street*, the next in Chastity Riley series, won the German Crime Fiction Prize. She lives in Sankt Pauli, in the heart of Hamburg, with her husband and son.

Follow Simone on her website: www.simonebuchholz.com.

ABOUT THE TRANSLATOR

Rachel Ward is a freelance translator of literary and creative texts from German and French to English, specialising in crime fiction and books for children and young adults. Having studied modern languages at the University of East Anglia, she went on to complete UEA's MA in Literary Translation. She has previously translated Simone Buchholz's *Blue Night*, *Beton Rouge*, *Mexico Street*, *Hotel Cartagena* and *River Clyde* for Orenda Books. Her translation of *Hotel Cartagena* won the 2022 CWA Crime Fiction in Translation Dagger award. Her non-fiction interests include history, politics, art, journalism and travel. Follow Rachel on Twitter @FwdTranslations, Mastadon as @FwdTranslations@zirk.us and Instagram as @racheltranslates.

THE ACAPULCO

SIMONE BUCHHOLZ

TRANSLATED BY RACHEL WARD

ORENDA BOOKS

Orenda Books
16 Carson Road
West Dulwich
London SE21 8HU
www.orendabooks.co.uk

First published in German as *Revolverherz* by Suhrkamp Verlag AG, Berlin 2021, in a
revised version of the text, reworked by the author, of the edition published in 2009 by
Droemer/Knaur, Munich, under the same title.

This edition published in the United Kingdom by Orenda Books 2023
Copyright © Suhrkamp Verlag Berlin 2021
English translation © Rachel Ward 2023

A catalogue record for this book is available from the British Library.

ISBN 978-1-914585-66-1
eISBN 978-1-914585-67-8

Typeset in Garamond by www.typesetter.org.uk

Printed and bound by CPI Group (UK) Ltd, Croydon CR0 4YY

The translation of this work was supported by a grant from the Goethe-Institut London

For sales and distribution, please contact info@orendabooks or visit
www.orendabooks.co.uk.

THE ACAPULCO

I saw her
she was walking down the street
her lips were red
she was wearing a dress
that wasn't pretty enough for her
for her face
for her walk
she was more
she was an idea
she went dancing
I watched her
she smiled at me
come with me
I said
and she came with me
and she fell asleep
and then we talked
and I made something of her

I KNOW, KID, I KNOW

The sky hangs low, it looks like it could use a lie-down. Fog rises from the Elbe, as tough and as mean as an old crow. I turn up my coat collar, but it's no use: the damp crawls into my bones. My head aches, I didn't get enough sleep. It's early March, it's only half past seven, and lying at my feet is a dead girl. Two Filipino sailors on shore leave found her.

She's lying on some steps that lead straight down into the water. She's naked, and there's a strangulation mark across her throat. Her breasts aren't the most elegant that money can buy, but they're pretty impressive. I wonder why she was laid out there so nicely and isn't swimming face down in the Elbe like all the other dead bodies. She's wearing a cheap, bright-blue, short-haired wig, I could do with a cup of coffee.

SOCO are in full swing. They've taped everything off, you're not allowed to put your feet anywhere, obviously; I've already been given a good telling-off for traipsing around down here, but I don't care, I have to see the victim if I'm going to take care of her.

Click.

Now they're taking photographs.

They always take photographs like crazy, and there are all these excitable little signs all over the place, as if there was something totally make-or-break here. I can't make anything out. Except wet cobblestones.

One of the lads, a skinny guy with a beaked nose, starts to focus on the dead girl's neck.

'Where's the CID got to?' he asks.

'They're on their way,' I say.

'Who's the murder-squad duty officer?'

'Chief Inspector Faller,' I say.

'That old plodder.'

'Hey,' I say, 'watch your step. And until Faller gets here, I'm the CID, got that?'

'Got that, Madam Prosecutor.'

He raises his eyebrows.

Arsehole.

Faller is very much OK in my book. Sometimes he might be a bit tired, but he's always there. And when something's eating him, he reminds me of Robert Mitchum. And then, to cheer him up, I say: 'My word, Faller, you're a cool cat. If I were twenty years older, I'd marry you on the spot.' His usual reaction is to stare at the ground, light a Roth-Händle and say: 'I know, kid, I know.'

I really am fond of him.

'How did she die?' I ask the SOCO man, while I try to make out individual clouds in the sky.

'Strangled,' he says, 'probably with something plastic, a cable or similar.'

'When?'

'Can't say precisely yet. Probably after midnight. The doc will be able to narrow it down a bit later.'

'OK,' I say. 'Anything else?'

'Oh, yes,' he says, lifting the wig a little.

Beneath the wig there is neither hair nor skin. There's just a crusted, bloody mess. All at once, I'm dizzy.

'Wow, she's been...?'

'Precisely,' he says, 'the lady's been scalped.'

There are a few aspects of my job that I don't deal so well with, and mutilated women are definitely among them. I put my hands on the back of my neck and check my hairline. All still there. I pull my coat tighter around my waist.

'Listen,' I say, 'I have to go. And leave Faller in peace when he gets here.'

Then I scram. Do not go and keel over on the crime scene, Riley.

I ONLY START TO GET LONELY IF THERE'S SOMEBODY THERE

The cobbles are damp and unpredictable beneath my boots. Better walk nice and slowly for once. I'm wondering why I keep doing this to myself, these crime scenes. Probably because I'd rather be outside than inside, because I'm not yet of an age when I can simply issue wise instructions, and maybe also because I don't really like my office at the State Prosecution Service. On good days it feels like a framework, and on bad ones like a jail. But maybe that's just the furniture. I should really deal with that.

Hey ho.

So, until something changes, I'll just keep going out. Besides which, I'm convinced that you have to see crime if you want to fight it. You have to know what evil looks like so that you'll recognise it when it crosses your path.

My phone rings. It's Faller.

'Good morning,' I say.

'Shitty morning,' he says. 'Where are you, Chas?'

'On my way to Carla's.'

'Coffee?'

'You know what a woman needs,' I say. 'Are you at the crime scene?'

'Yes,' he says, 'just arrived, along with the entire local press. They're turning everything upside-down here.'

'They need to back off.'

'I've got it under control,' he says. 'What d'you think of the wig?'

'What d'you think of the scalping?'

'Horrible, nasty, that poor girl.'

'Think she was a pro?'

'No idea,' he says. 'We should have the first results from forensics and pathology by tomorrow afternoon. I suggest we all meet up around two, and then we'll see.'

'OK,' I say. 'I'll talk to a few of the girls on Hans-Albers-Platz this evening.'

'Thanks,' he says. 'I'm too old for all that.'

'No problem,' I say.

Since an ugly incident a few years ago, Faller doesn't like getting out and about in the Kiez. I don't hold it against him. Everyone has their own shit to bear and all that. Something went wrong, it was a mistake, let's make the least-worst of it.

'I can send Calabretta to see the girls too,' says Faller.

Calabretta's family is Italian, and he's Faller's favourite on the murder squad; if you ask me, Faller wants him to succeed him one day. Fine by me. Calabretta's a good cop and a decent guy. But I'd rather talk to the ladies of the night myself. I've always liked having red light shining on my investigations, I like the people in the Kiez. It's an honest neighbourhood.

'Nah,' I say, 'it's fine, I'll do it. See you later at forensics, OK?'

'Sure thing,' he says. 'Oh, and Chastity?'

'Yes?'

'Take a double dose of aspirin and go and get some more kip. You sound awful.'

Faller is constantly worried that I might be in a bad way. He's mostly right.

I nod, not that he can hear that. He hangs up and I'm alone with the lump in my throat. When someone cares for me, it does me over.

The port is crazy busy. All the lights are on, there's rattling and clattering everywhere, cranes here, forklifts there, big commotion. I really prefer it when places are asleep, and the port in particular is somehow closer to me when it's quiet, by night. When the daytime no longer swallows up the lights. Still, the sun breaks through the clouds for a moment, adds a dash of emphasis, and blinks sympathetically down on the containers. But then the sky closes right back up, all that industry is surrounded by greyness again, slogs away to itself. To port, two beefy guys are busy with some kind of crates on a barge. They whistle as I walk past; I knew they'd do that and I flip them the finger.

'What's eating you, love?' says one.

The other asks: 'Out on the lash yesterday?'

Look who's talking. Bet they're personally acquainted with the inside of every beer glass in the city. Dickheads.

I'm still cold. The cold is like an elderly monster that's

eating me up from the inside. And it starts doggedly eating the moment the outside temperature drops below thirty degrees. Once, a few years ago, I went on holiday, flew halfway around the world, spent four weeks on Tahiti. The travel agent said it was always at least twenty-eight there. They weren't wrong. The weeks on Tahiti were the time of my life. It was warm, the people smoked Gauloises and drank Heineken all the time, and they played guitar and everyone spoke French, and I didn't even try to understand a thing. I was entirely alone and not the tiniest bit lonely. I only start to get lonely if there's somebody there. In that month on the island, not even a mosquito bit me. I could have carried on that way forever, but in the end, I wussed out and took my pre-booked flight back to my life.

Sometimes, people ask me where I get that from – feeling the cold so quickly. I don't think that's any of their business.

IN A SERIOUSLY BAD WAY

Carla must have been there a while: the place is warm and tidy. The front windows gleam like they've been freshly cleaned and the combination of delicate white plasterwork on the ceiling, sky-blue walls and wild raggle-taggle of old chairs, tables and chandeliers is, as ever, so inviting that I wonder how anyone ever manages just to walk past Carla's café. She comes towards me, my God, she's so alive. Now and again, when I wonder what kind of a woman my mother might have been, I wish she could have been like Carla. But a woman like Carla would never have abandoned her child.

My mother walked out when I was two years old, ran off with a colleague of my father's, a senior officer. Now Ruth Hinzmann lives in Richmond, Wisconsin, sometimes sends postcards, and is on to her third husband, a dentist. That's all I know about her, and, to be honest, it's quite enough. These days, I think it wasn't such a bad thing to have grown up without her. My father and I were a good team. He's the one I miss. He's the one who went too soon, not her.

'Hey,' Carla says, giving me a kiss on the cheek. 'Kicked

you out of bed again, have they? I'll put some lovely music on, OK?'

I nod. For Carla, lovely music means sad Portuguese music. She often says sadness is basically the same as beauty, they both hurt, and then she always smiles like she's made of caramel.

She's messing around with the CD player with one hand and the coffee machine with the other.

'You do want coffee, don't you?'

'Mm-hm,' I say. As usual, Carla is barely wearing a thing, a thin, little black dress, and a cardigan that slips off her bare shoulders with every movement. My hot-blooded friend is never cold. She runs at high revs, she constantly chafes at life, she doesn't even know what the cold is. Beneath her hands the machine steams and seethes and clatters, and then she sets a cup of her glorious coffee in front of me.

'So,' she says, 'before I forget, I've found you a man, you'll like him.'

'Oh yeah?' I say.

Carla really does keep trying. She's constantly setting up some amazing date for me with some amazing guy. And then I either don't turn up to the date, or I drink myself adrift and act so off that she's ashamed of me in front of the loser. But that's water off a duck's back to her, it doesn't seem to bother her, so she keeps on matchmaking.

'Yeah, he's GREAT,' she says. 'He's a man in a suit, but the good type, you know? Lovely grey temples, does something in the theatre. And he's single.'

'There's got to be something wrong with someone who lives alone at that age,' I say.

'You live alone,' she says.

'My point exactly,' I say, 'there's tons wrong with me.'

'He's widowed,' says Carla, putting on a geography-teacher look. Over the top of the Portuguese tinkling out of the speaker above me. She knows exactly how to soften me up.

'OK,' I say. 'When?'

'This evening. He'll come here. And if I shut at ten, you two can easily go on somewhere else. A change of scene is always good on a first date. Takes the pressure off, you know?'

My friend seriously has a screw loose.

'I can't this evening,' I say. 'There's a dead girl down at the port, and I need to ask around a bit on the streets.'

'Oh, shit, baby. Is it bad?'

'Murder's always bad, Carla.'

'Yes, sure, but is she just dead, or was she in a bad way first?'

For Carla, my job's just one big Saturday-night film.

'In a seriously bad way. She's naked and instead of a scalp, she's got a blue wig on her head.'

'Whoa, that's out there...' Carla is all big eyes and big breasts.

'Carla!'

'Sorry,' she says. 'But why do you always have to have such awful cases?'

'Because I'm responsible for awful cases, Carla.'

'Want something to eat?' she asks.

'No,' I say. 'Better not.'

I CAN'T BE DOING WITH FEAR

Carla forced me to eat a ham toastie. Sometimes, I wish she'd just have a baby so I'd be free from her solicitude. I still feel sick, and the hangover I ordered last night is slowly wandering in. My hands shake and the pain in my head has acquired a soundtrack. Serves me right for not heeding my dad's advice. He taught me everything he considered important, including the necessity for alcohol to be clear. I don't know myself why I was so set on drinking that dark stuff with the lizard on the bottle last night. I just felt like it, and the guy next to me at the bar liked it too, and after three glasses, he said, 'Ready when you are.'

'Ready for what?' I asked.

'We can talk now,' he said. By about half past three, everything had been said and the bottle was empty.

Now I can't find the keyhole and I'm wondering when the damn caretaker will ever get round to fixing the light on the stairs.

'Hey, look at that, it's my favourite neighbour.'

Klatsche's sitting on the grubby wooden staircase, playing the gigolo.

'Hey, look at that, where did you spring from?'

His shock of dark-blond hair could use another cut, it's falling over his forehead. His young face bears the traces of having grown up too soon, and he is, as always, sincerely unshaven. He spends the majority of his time driving women out of their minds, and he's pretty good at it, the little spiv. Klatsche has an impressive wide-boy career path behind him. He was fourteen when he first broke into a villa in Blankenese for a dare. He found it so easy that from then on he did it often, and by the age of sixteen he was earning good money selling electricals from his permanently sozzled parents' garage: TVs, stereos, computers, all off the back of a lorry. When he was seventeen, he got busted for the first time – didn't notice an alarm system. Six months later it happened again, there was a container full of music systems and someone grassed him up; he got nicked the third time when he was in the middle of emptying a warehouse of photocopiers – alone. He'd got cocky, wanted to be the famous burglar king. They gave him nine months. And since then, he gets anxious the moment a door closes behind him. He always says prison was the worst time of his life, that he never wants to go back there, no way, that he'd rather die than go back behind bars. He'd had it up to here with a life of crime. So he stopped with the burglary and set up as a locksmith. Business is booming. There's nobody quicker, cheaper or happier picking a lock.

'So why are you sitting around out here?'

'I lost my key.'

'Oh, please, Klatsche,' I say, 'there's no door in the world you can't get open...'

He grins and shrugs.

'No way,' I say.

'Yes way,' he says.

'Mr Locksmith extraordinaire went out without his kit?'

'A genuine emergency.'

I know what his emergencies look like: blonde, barely over twenty, striking statistics in the chest department.

'So all concerned are now exceptionally pleased that the nice neighbour has a spare key at her place, huh?'

Klatsche nods. He's got his going-out leather jacket on, a rancid brown thing with a broken zip, and looks like he hasn't had a shower today. An emergency, got you.

'Fine,' I say, once I've finally managed to open my own door. 'Come in.'

Klatsche peels himself off the step, stands up, waits three seconds on the threshold of my flat and looks at me.

'It's OK,' I say.

He puts his hands in his trouser pockets and takes a ridiculously cautious step into my hallway. I walk wordlessly past him into the kitchen. Klatsche was last in my flat six months ago. Since then, he's been strictly barred. Because that day, for reasons that I can no longer remember, he ended up in my bed, and we didn't get out of it for twenty-four hours. Not that it wasn't nice, quite the reverse. But I couldn't think, couldn't sleep, couldn't work for days afterwards, it threw me off course. That scared me, and I can't be doing with fear. Besides, the guy's a good fifteen years younger than me.

So.

I have the feeling that we're over that now, so I don't want to be like that.

He stands in the kitchen door, taps the doorframe with his finger, as if it's burnt him, and goes: 'Tsss...'

'Stop that shit, Klatsche, or I'll throw you out again. I'm old enough to be your mother.'

'But you're not, baby.'

'Don't call me baby.'

'What's happened?' He drops, wide-legged, onto a chair, I can see the muscles tense beneath his jeans. Outside my kitchen window, the clouds are piling up again, and slipping a little lower, they're almost lying around the backyard now. I tell him about the dead girl while I make coffee. About the wig and what was, or rather wasn't, under it.

'That was sad,' I say.

'Sadder than the grandad with no feet last winter?'

'Yes,' I say, 'much sadder. The feet thing was a straight-forward matter between Albanians. The grandad was punished for knowingly straying onto their patch. But this doesn't seem like it comes from breaking an agreement. This must be something else. Something sicker. Who steals a woman's skin and hair?'

'Shout if you need any help,' he says.

I could use some help, I think, although not the way you mean, but I'd rather not say so, that would only cause trouble.

When I'm through with a body, I'm in a bad place. With a body under your nose, you temporarily stop kidding yourself and realise: all this can all go wrong very fast. Don't feel too safe, it's all just an illusion, and even if you think that every catastrophe in your life has already happened, it can always get worse. The only thing you can do then is not pull anyone else in with you.

I try not to stare too hard at Klatsche's forearms.

'Here,' I say, putting a cup of coffee somewhat roughly under his nose.

I need to get him out of my flat as fast as possible. I must have overestimated myself.

SHOWTIME

As a child, if my dad sent me down into the cellar, I used to sing quietly to myself. Just quiet enough that I could still have heard if some faceless hunchback had loomed up on my left, but loud enough to delude the monsters. Now, as I walk towards forensics, I'd quite like to sing.

Faller's behind me on the stairs.

'Showtime!'

'Ghost train,' I say, waiting a moment until we're in step.

'How are you?' he asks, looking appraisingly at me. He's worrying again.

'I'm tired,' I say. 'And not in the mood for a second encounter with a mutilated woman.'

'Yes,' he says, 'somehow they seem even more threatening on the slab.'

'When you've seen them the second time, it's much harder to forget what they look like. Have you spoken to the two Filipino sailors?'

'Yes,' says Faller. 'They're acting like they're too shocked to speak. But I don't think they can know anything of interest to us. They don't seem the calibre we're looking for.

Besides which, their ship sails again this evening and there's no real reason to keep them here.'

Faller as ever. I think he's right and I trust his judgement. The old man will know how to assess the situation.

'And what do the SOCO guys have to say?'

'A fair bit,' says Faller. 'The upshot of which is that we don't have a single usable line on the perpetrator, not even a footprint. Rained cats and dogs again last night. The bloke was in luck with the weather.'

'What makes you so sure our murderer's a man?' I ask.

'Throttling someone,' he says, 'is not exactly a woman's thing, is it?'

We walk side by side down the last few steps, and the further down we get, the smoother and more sterile everything gets, the grey stairs and walls look so slippery that once you're down, you might as well forget ever making it back up.

'Everything OK?' Faller asks.

'Yes,' I say, 'everything's OK.'

Ahead of us there's the steel door to pathology, behind that is the plastic curtain, and behind that is what remains of a crime. I'd like to link arms with him but don't have the nerve.

Open door, curtain aside, dance of the dead.

The pathologist is washing his hands. By and by, I join in, and the moment I've finished here, I'll wash my nose out too. The disinfectant smell of these clinical catacombs makes me all jittery. Sweet and lemony, spilt Sicilian liqueur plus Domestos. And once you've smelled it, you can't get it out of your nose all day. Whatever I want to eat or drink later, it'll taste of post-mortem. Most days after a visit to the university hospital cellars, I just don't ingest anything else.

The room is fully tiled, and bathed in a greenish shimmer. The girl is lying under a neon light on the horrible, high dissecting table. Her skin is very white, almost transparent. Running around her neck is the imprint of her deadly encounter with a strangulation device, and a fraction further down, running parallel and at right angles to it, are two finely stitched, pale-reddish lines. One runs along her collar bones, one down from the little hollow beneath her voice box to her pubic bone. Opened, closed. The bright-blue wig is on a shelf between the wash basin and the table, packed up in a freezer bag. Her face is young, pretty, and almost a touch cheeky. I'd put her at mid-twenties, tops. Her skull is just one big disaster zone. I can barely look.

'Go ahead, doc,' says Faller.

This is our division of labour: in pathology, he basically does the talking while I try not to keel over.

'Death occurred between two and four a.m.,' says the doc. 'She was strangled and probably put up barely any resistance. We found very few skin particles under her fingernails and nothing that indicates a struggle. But she was drugged up to her eyeballs, a woman who could defend herself would be a different story. She was only scalped after death. The killer probably used a small, sharp blade to do it. And she didn't die where you found her. We still have a few analyses to do. I'll write it all up for you tomorrow.'

I catch another glimpse of the girl's skull and suddenly I can taste exactly what I had for breakfast. I hope the toast stays put.

DANCER'S FACE

Over the course of the day, this morning's fog has turned into a malicious drizzle, and, yet again, the sun didn't make it. It's just after nine. The girls are standing in a row, each with her very own square metre of space, and they're wearing their winter uniform: ski pants, thick anoraks in pastel colours and moonboots. It's all tight-fitting, and they have bum bags round their waists with their work gear in them. Money, keys, phone, condoms. Behind them is Hans-Albers-Platz with its purveyors of amusements, which have been offering the same combination of fast-drinking music and old, cheesy hits for years, and where half the population of Pinneberg comes to drink away its small-town boredom at the weekends. Blinking in the girls' faces are the sex adverts on the other side of the street. I always wonder who teaches them this look, this blend of seduction and rebuff. The look is important. It creates the correct power relationship between the whores and their clients: toe the line and pay in advance, or you're not getting any. But if you do – well...

Suza and Danila have been standing here forever. They want to stop in the autumn, they once said something about opening a tanning studio together. Suza wears apple green, Danila wears pink, their peroxide blonde hair is topped with black woolly hats. They're trying to keep warm by walking on the spot. Small, cowboy movements.

'Hey, good evening,' I say.

'*Moin*.'

'Well?'

'How's business?' I ask.

'Oh,' says Suza, 'you know.'

Danila: 'And you?'

'I need to ask you something,' I say. 'Do you have a minute?'

Nods.

I pull a photo of the dead girl, taken at the scene, from my coat pocket. One with the wig. If they know who she was, the shock will be bad enough.

'D'you know her?'

Danila takes the photo from my hand and shakes her head. I believe her. If these girls have anything, it's a sense of what matters.

Suza shifts position by precisely twenty centimetres, so that she can take a look too. 'So, I guess that means more like "knew her", huh?' she says.

'Where d'you get this girl, then?' asks Danila.

'The port,' I say. 'Early this morning.'

Suza studies the photo for quite a while. 'Well, she didn't work here at least. Never seen her before.'

'Not on Davidstrasse either?' I ask.

'Nope,' she says.

'You sure?' I ask.

Suza nods. 'Very sure.'

I put the picture away again.

'Where else might she have worked around here?' I ask. 'Any exciting new opportunities for entry-level positions?'

'I reckon she's got a dancer's face,' says Danila.

'Yeah,' says Suza, 'her type hang around the poles, not on the street. I'd ask around a few clubs if I were you.'

She looks up at the window above her head and to the left. On the first floor, someone's fiddling with the curtains. We're being watched.

'Call me if you hear anything?'

The women nod again.

'Thanks,' I say. 'Apart from that – everything OK with you? Need anything?'

'We're OK,' says Danila. 'Be nice if it warmed up a bit now though.'

Tell me about it.

'Got any cigarettes?' asks Suza.

I fumble with the packet, pull out four Luckies, and hand them to her. They look up to the window again, the one with the wobbly curtain, and there's a rather cramped line to their mouths now. I should go. If they talk to me for too long, there'll be trouble.

'Thanks,' says Danila. 'Give my love to Klatsche.'

'Will do,' I say.

I have an ominous feeling of vertigo.

Somehow, everything's the same as ever.

PIMPS, FOR EXAMPLE

Seen from the outside, our Prosecution Service building isn't all that bad. Classic Hamburg redbrick, large, venerable, formidable. But from the inside, the thing's a disaster. Nothing's been done to it since the eighties, and it was done pretty badly then. The corridors are pickled in grey, brown and PVC, the offices in racing green, orange and rubber tree. I hate my office. It's stifling, dusty and I can't think there. Ideally, I'd like to be a roving public prosecutor, if there were such a thing. Chastity Riley, always on the move. Bummer.

At least the sun's shining outside my window, making the bare trees and even the fundamentally somewhat affronted-looking penal facility opposite look quite good. Apparently, spring's due here imminently, or so they say on the news.

When I was a little girl, and even as a young woman, the cold didn't bother me. But there came a time, shortly after my father put a bullet into his brain, when my blood grew frosty and the pressure in my veins dropped off. I'd just turned twenty and been with friends in a bar in Frankfurt, we'd been drinking and dancing, and all the stuff you do when you just traipse through life without too many worries. Around half past two, I made my way back to our flat – I never called it 'home', the circumstances of my origins felt too complicated for that. My mother, the woman from Hanau, was in the USA, and my father, the man from the USA, was living in Frankfurt. I lived somewhere in between.

I unlocked the front door as quietly as possible – I didn't want to wake my dad. But when I stepped into the hallway, I could see a light on in his study. I reckon I must have said something like: 'Dad? Are you still up?'

I can't remember.

All I remember is that I was standing in front of his desk, not daring to touch the dead body. He'd slumped forward, his shot-up head in a pool of blood, his gun on the carpet, and in his left hand was a crumpled note asking me please to forgive him. Since then, my blood pressure's not been all that, and I'm always cold.

I walk from the window to the desk and light a cigarette. On the desk are piles of newspapers and files, the local paper for today has our girl on the front page:

'Harbourside Horror – Sick Killer Scalps Young Woman'

Next to the paper is my file on the case, with photos of the body. A few from pathology and a few more taken at the crime scene. I take a deep breath, sit down and look at them again. I try to focus on her face, but I keep seeing the thing that isn't there anymore. Judging by her eyebrows, she was a brunette, or not a pale blonde at any rate. I don't know why, but I imagine that she had long, glossy curls. Maybe because it's the greatest possible contrast to that weird porn wig.

I lay my cigarette in the ashtray, pick up a pen and a pad, because I want to make a list of questions to be answered, like you do in cases like this, but then I feel dizzy, put down the pen, hold on to the desk and take another hasty drag at my cigarette. Shut my eyes. I'm back in my mid-twenties, back doing my law degree, I wear my hair up in a neat bun, I'm conscientious, a good student, I do what people expect of me, I don't do it for me but for my dead father, he always longed for me to be cool and strong, to be successful, to show them all what's what, and that's exactly what I show him, I do everything right, every day.

These days, I'm not as hard on myself, or on everyone else who's just had bad luck.

Someone knocks on my door.

'Not now,' I say.

Someone pauses, I can almost hear them thinking outside. Then: departure. My secretary probably only wanted to bring me a cup of coffee like she always does at around this time, and I, stupid cow, let her go.

I breathe in and back out and take the file in my hand again. We've got nothing yet that could help us find out who the dead girl was. Not even a little porcelain crown on a broken tooth, or anything else that we could pester dentists' databases with. There's been nobody reported missing in the last twenty-four hours. And without the identity of the victim, there's no link to the killer, that's just how it is.

I call Klatsche.

'Hey.'

'Hey, Klatsche.'

'Baby. You sound awful.'

'Knock off the baby shit,' I say. 'Where are you right now?'

'At work,' he says. 'Super busy, apparently today is national Lock Yourself Out Day, or something.'

'Anywhere near the Kiez?'

'No-oo,' he says, 'but I can drive over. Is this about the dead girl?'

'Yes,' I say. 'Somebody needs to talk to a few people. We have no idea who she was.'

'I presume you want me to talk to the kind of people you don't like talking to so much.'

'Correct,' I say.

'Pimps?' he asks.

'For example,' I say. 'My colleagues are combing the dance clubs this evening, but I can't let them loose on pimps, that never works.'

'It's a bit early in the day right now,' he says, 'but I'll take care of it.'

'Call me if you find anything, OK?'

I hang up, take my coat and go out. Fresh air.

ANARCHO-ELVIS

I'm standing on deck and smoking into the wind. To my left are the container ships, cranes and remnants of old harbourside housing, to my right are the floating high-rises where people who've fled wars and death are forced to live. Glued on behind them is the city, looking massive, a silhouette made up of faint lights, like another facet of the cloudy sky. Sitting beside me is a woman, she's got headphones on and she's looking at the water. She's wearing a pale-pink skirt suit and looks like a businesswoman. She seems to have a bit of a problem with her shoes, her feet are kind of squidged up at the instep. And the music coming from her headphones must be perversely loud, punk rock at a guess. There's something appealing about the way she's sitting there in her suit and her too-small shoes with that din in her ears. I smile at her but she doesn't respond.

We put in at Museumshafen Övelgönne, there's a ship at the pier that's been turned into a café, and little old houses with tiny front gardens by the shore. I look over again at Ms Punk Rock – now she does suddenly smile but I don't think it's for me – and walk ashore.

The snack bar's still standing. It's so ramshackle and worn out that one day it'll be swallowed up by the water. It's a dream spot, but not many people know it. Most of them are sucked into the flashy cafés near the beach. You can't make out the snack bar's soul from the outside. It's not even a hut, more a hovel. But opposite is the heart of the port, there are the big docks, it feels good to have them so close. And the moment you're inside the place you can feel it: everything's OK here, you can even get pea soup on a really cold day. And it was here, a few years back, that I met Carla.

It was a Saturday, it was raining and stormy, and the shack was full to bursting, half the beach seemed to be there, seeking shelter from the weather. I was feeling lonely and had already walked around half the port looking for a bottle of beer. Carla happened to be standing beside me in the doorway, we were both trying to squeeze inside when, suddenly, a wave of Elbe water sloshed over the jetty. There were no ships in sight, the wave came up out of the blue, and after the initial shock everyone in the joint started to convulse with laughter, probably with relief that the old place hadn't just gone and jumped into the river with it as it left. Carla and I were the only ones to have been properly caught by the splash, and also the only ones not to be cracking up. I was seriously pissed off, my hair and coat were dripping wet, I'd swallowed brackish water, it was gross, I was almost on the point of yelling at everyone when Carla reached for her neighbour's fish roll, took out the herring and bit right into it so that half the thing was in her mouth. She tilted her head, pulled a silly face in my directions and, wet as she was, it looked savagely funny.

I ordered two beers.

Since that day, we've been friends. She's my only girlfriend.

Today there are only a few scattered figures standing around here, scruffy, old harbour men with satisfied, furrowed faces. One of them's got a guitar round his neck and is playing Elvis. He doesn't sing, just strums one song after another. On the blackboard behind the bar, it says *TODAY: CURRY-WURST. SO BIG THEY OUGHT TO BE BANNED.*

I call Faller and tell him he should come down here.

'Why?' he asks.

'There's anarcho-currywurst and Elvis,' I say.

'What else?' he asks.

'I could use some company.'

'OK, I'm coming.'

Quarter of an hour later, my colleague is here, maybe he put his blue lights on. Sometimes I suspect him of having secretly adopted me. But maybe that's just wishful thinking. His daughter is twenty now. When I see Faller with his daughter, when I see the way he stands up for her, whatever happens, when I see all the love for her in his eyes, a pair of pliers grips my soul and crushes me to smithereens, and sometimes Faller happens to notice that, and then he somehow draws me into the circle, and I could cry my eyes out and have to have a smoke.

I've ordered the monstrous currywurst-and-chips twice, and push one portion over to Faller.

'Beer?' he asks.

'I'm on duty,' I say.

Faller grins. He knows that I don't give a stuff about that and drink anytime, day or night, if I'm in the mood. But right now, I'm not in the mood, so I'm drinking apple juice. Detective Chief Inspector Faller orders himself a water. Since that shit that time, that gloomy night when the alcohol robbed him of his dignity, he doesn't touch a drop.

I bite into my currywurst. Hard on the outside, soft on the inside, just enough salt and a touch too much pepper.

'So,' says Faller, 'what's the dead girl doing in your head?'

'Lying around bleeding,' I say with a mouthful.

'Then we'd better turn her over a bit,' says Faller.

'I don't want to,' I say, skewering two chips.

'I'm afraid we can't take that into consideration just now,' he says.

He pops a lump of sausage into his mouth and closes his eyes as he chews. The man with the guitar is playing one of my favourite songs: 'Walk a Mile in My Shoes'. And I imagine the sky outside, over the docks, has taken on a rosy shimmer.

'I just can't focus on the case properly,' I say. 'My head won't start, and if it does, it hurts.'

'Where exactly does it hurt?' he asks. 'A dead body doesn't usually cause you this much difficulty.'

It's because he removed her skin, I think. I think about her skin and get scared for my own, for whatever reason.

'I can't get access to his brain,' I say. 'I can't and won't put myself into his shoes.'

Faller knows as well as I do that that's normally my great strength: thinking like the perpetrator. Deep down in my heart, I'm a criminal. A real bad guy. But not a psychopath.

'It's because you're not a psychopath,' says Faller.

'Are you?' I ask, downing my juice.

'I'm more the type,' he says, 'for an honest, straightforward murder.'

I know he is.

'So we're in a pretty shitty position,' I say.

'Nobody needs to know,' he says. 'And now, let's stroll arm in arm into hell.'

I put my plastic fork aside. Outside, a gust of wind whips around the corner of the hut and rattles its wooden boards, and then it's quiet again, apart from the gulls, until the next squall. The man with the guitar has stopped playing.

Faller dips three chips in the curry sauce and sticks them in his mouth.

'The idea of a skinned scalp,' he says, chewing, 'how bad is that for you?'

'I can't say.'

'Uh-uh,' he says, 'you can't talk about it.'

I shrug my shoulders.

'He didn't want her skin, Chas,' he says. 'He wanted her hair. And, unfortunately, he wanted it intact. So stop thinking about skin. The point at issue is hair.'

'I think she had brown hair,' I say.

'That's rubbish, Chas,' he says. 'There are loads of blondes with dark eyebrows.'

'Do we know anything about the wig?' I ask.

'Made in Australia,' he says, 'sold all over the world. Mass produced and available in any drag shop – there are hundreds on the shelves in the Kiez alone.'

Now I do order myself a beer, what the hell. And Faller demolishes the rest of his sausage and recites, through a full mouth, one of his favourite bits of poetry, it's a line from a very lovely song that I once played him years ago when he wasn't doing so well: 'Humans are mainly water and the rest is alcohol. If you can cry when drunk as a skunk, you'll feel complete and whole.'

'It's nearly two,' I say, taking a huge swig from the bottle. 'We have to go.'

PHENOBARBITAL, TWO CIGARETTES AND AN APPLE

Sitting around a large table in the Prosecution Service conference room are: Brückner and Schulle from Faller's murder squad; Borger, our forensic psychologist; a young junior pathologist; Hollerieth from forensics; Faller and me. Calabretta's not there, he had to take his mother to the doctor.

I like Brückner and Schulle. Classic Hamburg boys with flaxen hair and faces that never get any older than twenty-eight. Brückner is on the small side, and Schulle is on the tall side.

Borger's in his late forties, he's wearing very boring silver reading glasses and looks like the RE teacher next door, but speaks like a pro snooker player: chilled and serene. I've never known anything shake Borger out of his calm. My police colleagues call him Mr Valium, and I think he knows it; obviously, he doesn't care.

I don't know the pathologist, she seems to be new. She's strawberry blonde and has an impressively pointed nose, along Cleopatran lines, and at first glance she looks madly delicate, but at second glance she's very professional. Shame Calabretta isn't here. I reckon she could be his type.

Hollerieth is the forensics chief and among all these egg-heads, he's the one I like least. I have an actual need to hurt him. He's a supercilious type with a plump face and long, scrawny hands that are totally out of keeping with the rest of his appearance, and something about him drives me up the wall. Maybe just him being there is enough. Along with his plump face, he has an equally plump grey moustache, and he's wearing a rough grey jacket, a hideous patterned tie and a sloppy shirt.

'We have practically nothing,' he says, letting a reproachful look slip over the table. As if any of us could help that.

'Meaning what, exactly?' asks Faller.

Hollerieth opens his file, spidery-fingered and self-important.

'On Monday night, it bucketed with rain. As a result, we've got any number of footprints and tyre prints, but they're blurred and untraceable – any number of people go traipsing and driving about on the cobbles down by the port. We didn't find a single trace of foreign DNA on the corpse, just a few clothing fibres. Someone was probably wearing jeans and a woollen jumper, either her or the killer. And we are working on the assumption that she was strangled with a plastic cable because we have found no fibrous material around her neck.'

Hollerieth looks at the young pathologist. 'Would you agree?'

'Plastic,' she says with a nod. She has a beautiful, smoky voice that goes perfectly with her hair colour. 'But the injury makes me think it was more likely a cable tie than a cable. A cable wouldn't have left such a cut.'

'Anything else?' I ask. 'Was there anything under her fingernails?'

'Nothing that indicates a fight,' she says. 'All the skin particles we found were her own. She might have scratched her head, nothing more. The only bruising is the mark on her neck. And the livor mortis indicates with reasonable certainty that she was transported to the place where the two sailors found her after death.'

'What about the pills the doc talked about?' I ask.

'Phenobarbital,' she says, 'a strong soporific. It's prescription-only, and normally used either in preparation for an anaesthetic or to treat epilepsy. It's hard stuff to get hold of. It's possible, of course, that our killer is an epileptic. But then he'd need it for himself and couldn't afford to blow such a large dose of it.'

'What effect does it have?' Brückner asks.

I was just about to ask the same thing. These early team meetings are always a bit like your first lesson with a new maths teacher: everyone's trying to look as clever and attentive as possible.

'Depends on the dose,' says the doctor, whose way of speaking appeals to me more with every phrase she utters. An attractive, detached sing-song. I'll have to ask Faller if he got her name. 'The victim was given a decent amount mixed with gin,' she says. 'I think she fell asleep on her feet and was then hastily sent the way of all flesh. Phenobarbital is powerful stuff, you wouldn't need to do much to help it along.'

'The killer didn't want to hurt her,' says Borger, scratching his chin.

'And she won't have felt a thing,' says the doctor.

'My hunch is that he killed her first and then undressed her,' says Mr Borger. 'Our man doesn't seem particularly daring to me, he wanted to be on the safe side. If she'd had the slightest chance of defending herself, he wouldn't have been able to go through with his plan. That would fit with the cable tie too. You just have to pull it good and tight and then you can let go, the rest does itself.'

'The cut to remove her scalp was also done after death, and carefully, not brutally,' says the pathologist. 'He worked with a sharp but smallish blade. Possibly a carpet knife.'

'I don't think he's the kind who hate women,' says Borger. 'He might not even know what he's done.'

'Did he have sex with her?' I ask the doctor.

'No,' she says. 'There was nothing of that type.'

'Wouldn't have fitted,' says Borger.

'Can you tell us anything else about the kind of person we're dealing with here?' I ask him.

He stretches. 'I'm sure it's a man,' he says, 'and I don't think he's particularly old. We might not even be talking about a man, but a boy. Or if he is older, then he's only halfway to emotional adulthood. Such things happen when something breaks, something erupts, something that's been simmering a long time and suddenly can't be contained within the oven of the soul. And it generally breaks out when a person takes a step in their development. But that's more just my feeling.' He knits his brow and looks at me. 'I'd say we're looking for a rather unobtrusive, nice guy, possibly even a very charming man. There must have been a reason why the woman went with him.'

Schulle exhales loudly. '"Our neighbour was always so kind and so shy, we'd never have thought it of him"?'

Borger shrugs and starts filling his pipe.

Faller eyes his two guys.

'Have you two found anything to identify the victim yet? Do we have even a lead?'

Brückner shakes his head, his face is all crumpled.

Schulle leans back in his chair, arms crossed.

'We haven't got through all the dance clubs yet,' he says, 'and I reckon there's a heap more clubs we don't know about – unofficial ones. It'd be nice if we could get a bit of help from the vice squad or something.'

'There's a friend of mine,' I say, 'who's happy to help, and I've pretty much already sent him out.'

'That's good too,' says Schulle.

Brückner looks a little put out. He's not keen on other people getting involved.

'That's OK,' says Faller, 'we've often worked with the young man in question.'

People are starting to stand up, so that's that then, every-one hangs around the table a bit, sneaks a look at other people's files, and I discreetly approach the pathologist with the raspy voice.

'Ms Riley,' she says, 'nice to meet you at last.'

'Really?'

I give her my nicest smile.

'I'm Bettina Kirschtein,' she says. 'But my friends call me Betty.'

'Do you smoke, Betty?'

'Sometimes,' she says.

We go outside for a smoke, she pulls an apple out of her pocket and eats it to go with the cigarette. She says she always does. And she says it's fine by her if you hate pathology.

I'M HERE FOR THE EMOTIONS

In half an hour the home game will kick off. Carla and I meet, as we always do, on the south stand, she's got the beer, I've got the cigarettes. She's wearing her spring uniform: black pirate headscarf instead of a brown woolly cap, death's head sweatshirt instead of a thick jacket and Millerntor scarf.

'Isn't that a bit cold for ninety minutes?'

'Rubbish,' she says, 'it's at least twelve degrees. C'mon, gimme a fag.'

'Gimme a beer,' I say, and we make a quick prisoner exchange. The pitch is at our feet, at the other end is the north stand with the fashionista fans, and behind that the old grey bunkers towers against the evening sky. The floodlights feign illumination and the broken speaker system is clattering with hideous dad rock. It's fundamentally awful, but we love it. And it's already getting us down to think that there's going to be a football World Cup in Germany this summer. They'll convert stadiums into arenas, to make it all nice and smart for guys like Ronaldinho, brutal tackles will be pushed out by undersoil heating, and Franz Beckenbauer will do a deal with God: four weeks of glorious sunshine during business hours in return for no summer for the next three years. We all know that's what's going to happen.

The players are warming up. Carla and I obviously have our favourites. I like the tall midfielder, number seventeen – he's a colleague. A detective who's a good enough footballer to have a side-line on the local third-division team as well as his work on the CID. When he scores, the entire red-light district roars a cop's name – it's totally nuts. Carla prefers the young defender with fourteen on his back. She says he always knocks people down 'so charmingly'. We both find the goalie difficult. He comes from deepest Bavaria and I consider him a dense and chronically overrated bore. If you ask me, it's well past time for him to hang up his gloves. Carla says he's a lousy show-off and has no manners. The guy on benefits who always stands next to us takes a sporting view: 'He saves the unsavable stuff, but lets the ordinary, everyday stuff through every time. Hell, I don't get it.'

He doesn't get a lot of things. Recently, he asked me at half-time how it was possible that his wife had run off with a prostitute from Billstedt just because he'd messed around with that little Russian now and again. I couldn't help him there. But when you've stood tight-lipped next to someone for years, you kind of like them, so I nodded moderately sadly along to his story.

Carla is already cheering our boys on. She reckons they need support during the warm-up too. Sends them into the dressing room in a totally different frame of mind, she says.

I always spend the time before the match looking at the screwy ultras at the far end. They use the time to warm up their singing voices, get shit-faced and show each other the wild banners they're going to unroll shortly. I can't yet make out what's on this one but it's sure to have something to do with the chairman, who they always want rid of. I don't care, I'm here for the emotions.

The players are starting to trudge towards the dressing rooms. Carla breaks off her victory chants to say: 'The suit guy was in the café today.'

'So?' I ask.

'He was still looking like he could use a woman.'

'But I don't look like I could use a man, Carla.'

She glances up at me. Bambi-like.

'Forget it,' I say.

'He's really good!' she says.

'Then you have him,' I say.

'Not an option...' she says, looking at her feet.

'Carla, don't tell me Fernando's back on the scene.'

She pouts with her lips.

'Oh, man,' I say.

Fernando has been Carla's on-off lover for years, he's a massive arsehole and must be dynamite in bed – he makes her cry but she can't keep away from him.

'What about the suit guy?' Carla asks. 'Shall I fix something up?'

'No fucking way.'

Carla takes my hand. Then the players run on again, to a

gong and 'Hells Bells' by AC/DC. They jump, they wave, they slap their own cheeks, they make themselves fierce, the ground flips out, it's so loud, tickertape goes flying, flares burn, it's massive.

'If only they were as dangerous as they make out,' I say.

'Bollocks to that,' Carla says.

APPOINTMENTS, APPOINTMENTS

'Chas, where are you?'

'In the bath.'

'What's it smell of?'

'Nutmeg.'

'I gave you that one.'

'I know, Klatsche.'

'Good. Then jump out of the bath and into your clothes. You've got an appointment.'

'What do I have, when, where and with whom?'

'An appointment,' he says, 'at half past ten. At the pier by the old Fish Auction Hall. Guy named Basso. Just a small fish, but he reckons he might be able to help you.'

'Are you coming too?' I ask.

'I'll be at the door in ten minutes.'

I submerge again, listen to the water for a moment, re-emerge, step out of the bath, dry off, tie up my hair and pull on some jeans, a dark roll-neck jumper and boots. I take my coat, my hat, my cigarettes, open my desk drawer and look at the gun. It was my dad's. I'm not meant to have it, let alone use it, but it isn't really a gun, it's an heirloom, a memory.

And if I go out at night to meet a jobbing pimp, then I like to go equipped.

THE COBBLES ARE WET AND SMELL
OF FISH SKIN

Standing on the street are a couple of lads in brown
hoodies. They're swaying impressively and singing St Pauli
songs. Klatsche's leaning against his old Volvo, smoking
and looking at me.

'You look dangerous,' he says.

'You're very cute too.'

I open the passenger door and get in. The Volvo is a tip. If
I had a beauty like this, I'd keep it in good shape, but then
it's none of my business. Klatsche scrunches it into first. If I
were the gearbox, I'd be screaming, but I'm not. I watch him
sidelong for a touch too long, he looks back and raises his
eyebrows, then we pootle down our road. At night in particular, I sometimes suspect that we live on a stage set. All the
little shops, the half-heartedly renovated Jugendstil houses,
the adorably dirty bars, the fairy lights, the wonky cobblestones, the old trees, the ice-cream shop, the drunks, the
rubbish. Beautiful.

'How was the match?' Klatsche asks.

'Great,' I say.

'Did you win?'

'Yes,' I say. 'Just, and didn't deserve it, but all the nicer for that, a massive party atmosphere.'

'You hooligan,' he says.

Klatsche thinks third-division football's stupid.

We turn left then right, cross Simon-von-Utrecht-Strasse, which is something like Sankt Pauli's main road. The Reeperbahn looks lost in mid-week, and it's cold. We drive past the Davidwache with its blue neon *Police* sign and turn down Davidstrasse, but stop at a red light halfway along.

'What kind of guy's this Basso then?' I ask.

'Five-mark pimp,' says Klatsche. 'Little show-off. Likes to act important. But that suits us OK, doesn't it?'

I wind down the window and light a cigarette.

'Don't smoke so much,' says Klatsche.

'Want one?' I ask.

'Hand it over.'

I give him mine and light another for myself. The light goes green, he puts his foot down and I secretly watch him as he smokes and drives. His face is constantly flipping between two ages: when he drags on the cigarette, it looks striking and adult, when he blows out the smoke, he has the face of a schoolboy.

We drive along Davidstrasse with its squat little buildings; front-left of us we can see from far off the site where they're dragging up an enormous hotel. The girls on our right might be the most beautiful prostitutes in the city. They're haggling over prices and offers with drunk and probably desperate tourists. I look out of the window to the sky, the city lights add a dash of orange to the blue-black. We judder over the cobbles, both have our elbows on the arm rest, and Klatsche's arm is incessantly clicking against mine.

'Crappy potholes,' he says.

I can't see any potholes, the street's in very good shape for such an old lady, the showpiece of the Kiez. I pull my arm a little way away from his. He slides further over to me. I can feel his forearm against mine in no uncertain manner, a permanent miniature electric shock. I ignore it and concentrate on the road, which makes absolutely no sense for a passenger.

At the end of Davidstrasse, we turn left. There's the port, down there on the right, and, as it does every time, it suddenly looms up out of the darkness, I catch my breath for a moment. The port took me by surprise when I came to Hamburg ten years ago, I hadn't expected to find much more than a job here. I just wanted to get away from Frankfurt for a while, and the Hamburg State Prosecution Service was the first to offer me a position. I was intending to stay two, maybe three years, and then I wanted to go to Berlin. I didn't know anybody here, all I had was myself and my bad mood. But it didn't turn out like that. A city is like football: you don't choose your team. Your team chooses you. The port always reminds me of that whenever I'm on the point of forgetting to be grateful for it.

Klatsche stops in a dark corner outside the Fish Auction Hall. Brick buildings tower up on our right, almost every building has a kind of sluice arrangement on the ground floor. That's supposed to keep the Elbe at bay. The buildings look like the castles of the industrial revolution, with draw-bridges and everything, the cobblestones are wet and smell of fish skin.

'You're meeting down on the pier,' says Klatsche, 'and I'll always be at hand.'

'I'm not afraid.'

'I know,' he says. 'But it sounds good to say that.'

I give him a slap on the back of the head, he says 'thanks' and I make my way down the jetty towards the water.

It's twenty-five past ten, and it's blowing a gale. Opposite me, the industrial romanticism is blinking and wheezing, furtive and low key, in night mode. I turn up the collar of my trench coat, shove my hands in its pockets, keep walking slowly towards the water, trying to adjust to the sway and the slippery wood beneath my feet. As always at this time of night, I'm a little dizzy, I want to be on reasonably good footing when this Basso turns up.

But this Basso doesn't turn up. Not at half past ten, not at quarter to eleven. There's nothing here at all but the deep smacking of the water against the pier.

Although.

I feel like there's something over there on the left, behind the grey electrical box for the service vessels, as if something flitted, something crouched. Something large and black, something ugly, nasty. It's more a smell than anything I really saw, more of a sense. I wonder about creeping along and having a look, but no. You can easily fall into the water down here, and it's cold and the Elbe is full of tricky currents. I concentrate on my breath and try not to pay any attention to what I'm imagining in the corner behind the box, even if it's heavy and cold on the back of my neck. There are some shadows that you only think you see, in reality they're not actually there. A shadow is nothing more than a fear.

'Come on, Basso,' I say, 'come on.' I look at my watch. It's just before eleven. I could swear that something moves behind the grey box.

CUTE AREA

At twenty past eleven, Klatsche strolls down the jetty.

'Hey, I happened to be passing.'

'Stop that shit.'

'Well,' he says, 'our informer meet-up worked out perfectly.'

I light a cigarette.

'Reckon he saw me?' Klatsche asks.

'No idea,' I say. 'But I've got a bad feeling. Something's not right here. And something moved behind that electricity box there.'

Klatsche checks out the dark corner.

'There's nothing there,' he says, 'just the usual litter.'

I'm sure there was something. I'm not an idiot.

'Do you know where Basso lives?'

'No, but I can find out.'

Klatsche walks a little way along the jetty and calls someone. I can't hear what he's saying, the water's slapping loudly against the jetty and the wind's got up, but I can see him constantly nodding, scribbling a few numbers on the palm of his hand in an unwieldy yet pragmatic way, and then calling the next person. This goes on for a while.

Him standing there.

Him silhouetted against the night, him with the phone jammed between shoulder and chin, his neck muscles moving. I can't help looking over the whole time, and I almost jump when he's suddenly standing in front of me again.

'OK,' he says, 'let's go.'

'Where?'

'Hammerbrook. Spaldingstrasse.'

'Cute area,' I say, pulling my cap a bit lower over my face.

'Almost as cute as you, gun-face,' he says. 'And chuck that fag away, you smoke like a bloody chimney.'

SACK & SONS

We park the Volvo right beneath the S-Bahn bridge.
Hammerbrook, you'd have to be deeply in love to still find it
romantic. I was in love here for one night, when I was standing
on the roof of an empty skyscraper, I was drinking cheap red
wine. It was summer and warm, buzzing beneath me was the
main station. The man next to me had a pirate's heart and was
holding mine in his hand. In that moment, I might have quite
liked to leave it there, but in the end, I bailed before sunrise.

We get out, Klatsche locks the car.

'Don't just stand there like a lemon,' he says, walking round
the Volvo, taking me by the hand and running with me over
the road. A car races through behind us and I can feel it in
the back of my knees. If we'd run a step slower, we'd have
been run over.

'Are you trying to kill me, Klatsche?'

'The opposite,' he says. He's still holding my hand and
pulling me nearer to him. Each time I stand so close to him,
I realise how tall I am. If I stretched a bit, I could ruffle his
hair, and he's almost six foot three. In a strange way, he makes
me pay attention to myself. I disengage myself.

'Which block?'

'Number two, sixth floor,' he says.

We're standing right outside it.

Klatsche pulls out his skeleton key, fumbles with the lock a bit, the door clicks open. We leave the light off, get into the lift, take it up to the sixth floor and find two entrances. I light up each door with my lighter. One has a sign reading *Sack & Sons*, the other is blank.

'We'll take this one,' says Klatsche, getting to work on the unsigned door. Fumble, clack, snap. Open.

He really is fast.

Behind the door is a long corridor with ugly carpeting. I can feel through my boots how scratchy this floor must be. From outside, a cold streetlight shimmers through the window, an S-Bahn train passes by. To the left: three toilets, one for gentlemen, two for ladies. To the right: a kitchenette. This isn't a flat, it's a former office.

We walk slowly down the hall and reach a large room where there's a table but no chairs. Writhing beside the table is an offended rubber tree.

'You too can live like this,' says Klatsche.

'No, you can't,' I say.

It's quiet here, in an oppressive way. The space opens up into another room over there, the door is ajar.

So far, all I can see is a chair on its side, but I know that there's more waiting for us. Klatsche leads the way. He pushes the door open with his foot and kicks aside the chair.

'Shit,' he says.

I put the light on and ask: 'Is that Basso?'

Klatsche nods.

That was Basso.

You can't make out much of his face, his clothes are drenched in blood, his arms and legs twisted in all directions. Someone went to town there. More than one person, probably. His nose and chin are a well-stirred porridge, various unfriendly metal implements were involved. Professional work. I feel sick, it smells of death. Looks like Basso had something quite important to say. Klatsche has knelt down beside the poor bastard.

'Don't touch anything,' I say, putting my hand on his shoulder.

'Should I get out of here?'

'No,' I say, 'better stay. Otherwise the forensics nerds will just ask silly questions.'

For a while, we're both very quiet. Then I pull out my phone and call my colleagues.

Klatsche stares at me as if he wants to hold tight to me with his eyes, and I stare back. It's like there's a power flowing between us that's sometimes helping him and sometimes me, and as a result we can bear standing here unable to do anything more.

Seven minutes later, they're all there. Faller looks tired and doesn't say much. He just keeps shaking his head. We both know: let's talk about this tomorrow.

'That's how life is,' says Klatsche, once we're sitting back in the Volvo, 'for once in your life you want to act the big shot and they smash you to a pulp.'

I can't think of much in reply. I've seen it so often, these poor sods who smell their chance and then go right under the wheels.

'Could you call a couple of colleagues of mine in the morning?' I ask, to distract him.

'Sure,' he says, wiping his nose. 'Who?'

'Brückner and Schulle. They need intel about dance clubs on the Reeperbahn.'

'Ha, then I'm the guy they need!' he says, a little too cheerfully. He's making sure I can't see his face as he gets into gear and puts his foot down.

Later, around four in the morning, I'm sitting on the wooden floorboards in my living room, drinking beer. I know that Klatsche's doing the exact same thing, there's only a wall between us. I can feel my soul within me, constantly beating against my skin. If I had balls in my trousers, I'd call him over.

I GUESS THAT MUST BE A TOURIST HOTSPOT

This morning, I was in court, first trial day for a nasty little ring of drug dealers. Just the type of guys I can't be doing with. Stupid utter arseholes. Pushing crack and heroin on a grand scale, ideally to the child prostitutes in St Georg. No decency, no empathy, no heart. They don't even speak in complete sentences, just scraps – no, they don't even speak at all, they bark. And grin at me the entire time I'm reading out the indictment. I want them to be put away for a good ten years. Fingers crossed.

Meanwhile, Faller's been in pathology. Poor Basso got his skull smashed in. Forensics say there must have been two of them. Armed with clubs and knuckledusters. Kiez classic.

I kick a few stones as I walk down Hafenstrasse. I like this road, these few brightly painted houses with the hint of a front garden and an Elbe view; in the eighties, there were wild scenes here, large, burning images. Now Hafenstrasse's no more than a tourist hotspot, a place they make a massive deal of but where there's absolutely nothing happening these days. Germany just rides past a couple of times a day in the city sightseeing buses, looks out of the window for a moment, goes, aha, this is where it kicked off, things were exciting here once, before all the excitement moved to Berlin, oh, wow, it's really quite small isn't it? And then Germany's gone again. I think you could live here wonderfully unnoticed.

The sky is cloudy, it's cold but at least it's not raining. Northern Germany in March, only a few degrees above zero, it could snow again at any time. I light myself a cigarette, take two drags then throw it away again because it immediately makes me dizzy, then head to the chemist to get something for my blood pressure.

RESERVED AS A RENTED PARKING SPACE

Carla's set me up. I'm sitting in her café with a glass of white wine standing in front of me, while leaning on the bar beside me is the guy she picked out for me. He's wearing a well-cut, pale-grey suit. Actually, he's not that bad. Tall, around fifty, somewhat greying hair, slightly thinning but swept back in an old-fashioned way. And a self-assured face that doesn't give away his thoughts even for fifteen cents. He's sometimes looking at his coffee and sometimes at me. Carla's watching us out of the corner of her eye. I clear my throat.

'Got a cold?'

'No,' I say, meeting his eyes. They have a cold gleam. He holds my gaze.

'Nice café,' he says.

I say nothing and twizzle my wineglass in my hand a bit.

'I haven't been in Hamburg long,' he says, then lowers his voice a little. 'And I'm discovering a new beauty every day.'

Oh, that was a bit smarmy.

He drains his coffee and holds out his hand: 'Claudius

Zandvoort. I'm a guy who badly needs another coffee. Would you like one?'

'Thanks,' I say, 'but I'll stick to the wine,' and take his hand. 'Chastity Riley.'

The hand is dry and cold. He orders more coffee, we relax and chat inconsequentially about this and that, category: weather. He tells me he's been in town for six months. That he's the new artistic director at the Okzidental, a small Kiez theatre – a venerable institution but a bit run down, the Ministry of Culture want it knocked back into shape. I don't know. The place is somewhere between light entertainment and musicals. You can't make too much of a show out of that. I wonder why someone so certain of himself would take on that kind of job. All in all, I find him odd. He's as reserved as a rented parking space, but still flirting with me.

When he takes his coat and leaves, I get a feeling that we'll see each other here again tomorrow lunchtime.

Carla's playing around with her fingernails and grinning.

'Whatever you want to say, save your breath,' I say, looking out of the window a bit, watching the publishing and advertising people who are strolling through the Portuguese quarter, whiling away their slim lunchbreaks. Carla takes a cup of hot chocolate and a slice of cake to a table. When she returns, she puts her hand on my shoulders.

'Claudius Zandvoort,' she whispers.

'Stop it,' I say, stroking a stray hair out of her face. She's so soft again today. Sometimes I could snuggle up into her.

'What's wrong?' she asks. 'You like him, don't you?'

'He's OK,' I say. 'There's something else on my mind.'

'What?'

'Yesterday, two guys beat a minor-league pimp to death. Seems like he wanted to get something off his chest,' I say.

Carla's eyes take on a watery sheen. She crosses herself and says: 'You should eat something. I'll make you a quick cheese sandwich.'

Carla has a sensationally natural relationship with life and death.

My phone rings.

Faller.

'We know who she was.'

'Who?' I ask, my heart pounding. Carla presses the sandwich into my hand.

'A dancer. Your girls were right. Last night the guys traipsed round the rest of the joints in the area, and the barman at the Acapulco recognised her from the photo. She hadn't been there long. Her flatmate has identified her since then. I've just been to pathology with her.'

ANY NEW MEN

She has glossy black hair and a finely cut face, she's wearing overly tight brown pinstriped trousers, a pale jumper, a denim jacket with a pink faux-fur collar and can't be more than late twenties. Taut beneath her jumper are huge silicone breasts.

'Would you like a coffee?'

'No,' she says quietly, 'no thank you.'

'Chastity Riley,' I say, 'I'm the state prosecutor for the case.'

'Tatjana Schlicke.'

Her fear is hard to bear.

'I'll be right with you,' I say, and meet Faller at the coffee machine.

He looks tired.

'Hey,' I say.

'Hey.'

It really gets to him when he has someone in his office who's just suffered a loss.

'She came from Cottbus,' he says. 'Lost her job on a supermarket checkout six months ago. Her flatmate then got her the work in the club.'

'Any family?' I ask.

'There seems to be an aunt back east, but they weren't in contact.'

'How old was she?'

'Twenty-four.'

I grip the coffee machine. Twenty-four.

'What's their flat like?' I ask.

'Three rooms in Altona,' he says. 'Calabretta and SOCO are on their way over.'

I kick the machine and get myself a coffee.

'What was the dead girl's name?'

'Margarete,' says Faller. 'Margarete Sinkewicz.'

'Meet you at the car in ten minutes, OK?' I say, but what I actually mean is: Margarete. Nice name. Poor girl.

Faller nods, absently.

Meanwhile, Margarete Sinkewicz's friend is sitting there, tiny on her chair, utterly motionless. When she sees me, she raises her head.

'Maggie never hurt a fly,' she says.

'I know,' I say.

'I miss her,' she says.

I know that feeling too, I think, holding out a cigarette. She sticks it in her mouth, I give her a light.

'Did you notice anything about your friend recently?' I ask. 'Did she meet any new men or anything?'

'No,' she says, dragging on her cigarette. 'Nothing. There was nothing like that. We're not like that. We might dance in the guys' faces but we don't shag around. Least of all

Maggie. She never went out with anyone. Hadn't been on a date in ages.'

'OK,' I say, 'well, we'll need to have a bit of a look around your flat. One of the officers will drive you home later, but first you'll have to answer a few more questions.'

She nods, smokes. I give her my card.

'Call me if anything comes up,' I say.

She stares at the card.

'Any time, OK?'

'You've got a funny name,' she says.

'My father was American.'

She smiles at me as if she can see right inside me and as if to say: outsiders like us have to stick together. I smile awkwardly back.

PILLOWS, RUMPLED IN A NICE WAY

The girls' flat is on the ground floor of one of those sweet, low-rise buildings on one of those classic Altona streets. Super nice and oh-so cosy, but I think it would really get on my tits. The place looks like two students live here, as innocent as cookies, and there isn't the least hint that its residents earn a living with erotic dancing. The furniture's a mix of IKEA and cheerful bric-a-brac, there are curtains of glass beads and chains of fabric daisies in the doorframes, the windows onto the street are aslant and the sills are covered with supermarket orchids. I walk over to the living-room window and push a few flowers aside. Outside, the sun is shining.

Faller's hanging about in the hallway.

'Is there anything unusual here?' I ask.

He points to the skirting board. There are about forty pairs of killer heels standing there, a proper battalion of fuck-me shoes.

'Nothing unusual about that, Faller.'

'No? It seems like rather a lot of shoes to me.'

'Forty pairs between two young women, professional dancers,' I say. 'I call it perfectly ordinary.'

'How many pairs of shoes do you have then, Chas?'

'Three.'

He raises his left eyebrow.

I do too.

Calabretta's in the bedroom with forensics, so I say a quick hello.

He's almost a head shorter than me, he's unshaven and stands around legs wide apart, like a gangster. His parents come from the Naples area, moved to Hamburg in the sixties. Sometimes, when I look at him like this, I wonder what would have become of him if he hadn't grown up in Altona. And sometimes I think that, if he hadn't, he might have been on the other side today.

'Hey, boss,' he says. 'Long time no see.'

'True,' I say. 'You been on holiday?'

'Visiting my family in Campania.'

'Nice,' I say. Family. 'How's your mother doing?'

'Oh, well, you know,' he says. 'She has constant chest pains of some kind. The doctor says there's nothing really there. She says it's because my father keeps checking out other women. My father says there's never been anything in it, and anyway, at his age, he says, what would they even ... And I believe him, but sorry, gee, didn't mean to talk your ear off...'

He strokes his hair back with his hands and bites his lip. Calabretta loves his mother with an intensity that only an Italian can manage.

I envy him.

The girls must have shared a bed as there's only one. It's

unmade and the pillows are rumpled, in a nice way. Forensics are going through the bedside-table drawers.

'Go a bit easy, yeah?' I say. 'There's still somebody living here.'

General mumbling. Lying on the bedside table is a scrap of paper with a phone number scribbled on it.

'Can I take that?' I ask, pointing a finger at it.

Collective nodding. I say goodbye to Calabretta, take the paper, press it into Faller's hand and forget about it.

WE'LL BE IN THE RIVER IN A MINUTE

Faller and I are sitting in his patrol car. I'm smoking, he's looking for Italo pop on the radio. I know that's what he's looking for, he always does, he just loves it. To his pleasure, he finds Umberto Tozzi. My phone rings.

'Hello?'

'Hello, Patschinski here.'

Oh, lordy. The local press.

'Hello, Mr Patschinski,' I say.

'I hear there's news about the dead prozzie down at the port.'

Wow, he speaks about women with such respect. But hey, it sounds like he's got a bad cold.

'She wasn't a prostitute,' I say.

'What about the guy they made mincemeat of? He was in the trade though, wasn't he?'

I hold my breath for a moment and pull myself together.

'Five p.m.,' I say, 'press conference at police HQ.'

'Bit late for us,' he says.

'Stop moaning, Patschinski. You have a late edition, don't you.'

He doesn't answer. He lights a cigarette.

'And you should smoke less,' I say. 'Go back to bed, you're ill.'

'I'm not ill,' he says, 'I've got hay fever and smoking relieves the symptoms.'

I hang up.

Faller fishes in his trouser pocket for a Roth-Händle, which he sticks in his mouth.

'Can you see the sun, Faller?' I ask.

He nods.

'Want to go for a walk?'

He nods again. 'Elbe?'

'Seeing as we're here,' I say.

Faller grins. We're basically always at the Elbe. He drives a little way, takes the righthand bend down to the port with elegance, and then we get out and smooth down our coats simultaneously. What funny intersections we have.

I walk around the car and hook my arm into his, then we stroll over the cobbles towards the water, here a ferry terminal, there a fish wholesaler and yet another sushi restaurant. We march at a brisk pace towards the riverbank, Faller's going hell for leather, I'm always on the point of stumbling.

'We'll be in the river in a minute.'

He stops abruptly, shuts his eyes, shoves back his hat and lets the sun shine on his face. We're very close to the water. There's only a low railing separating us from the Elbe.

'Faller,' I say, 'we have to talk about that Basso.'

No answer.

'You know,' I say, 'the little pimp, yesterday, in Hammerbrook.'

'I don't want to,' he says.

'Why not?' I ask.

'Not in the mood.'

I look at him from the side. He doesn't react, just keeps playing the sun worshipper. Have a great time in pensioners' paradise, I think, and I'm about to say something, to explain to him that it's our damn job to talk about Basso, but then a ray of sunshine gets hold of me, hits me in the middle of the forehead, and I realise that my old colleague is right. That at this moment, nothing is more important than just staring at the sun in peace.

Faller again. The guy's dynamite.

SERIOUSLY SMEARY

Everyone at police HQ is freaking out over a bomb threat. Someone phoned and said he was going to blow up a U-Bahn station. So only buses are running for the moment, and there's a production line going checking out likely suspects. The riot police are marching out in their hundreds, they're setting up task forces, we're planning a major raid. Obviously, they're just following protocol, but in the end, it's only going to be yet another guy who got bored and happened to stroll past a phone box. Sometimes I'm glad the only public transport I take are the river ferries and that otherwise I always walk or let Klatsche or Faller drive me.

I stand around feeling slightly lost and not quite knowing what to do with myself. I feel like I'm in the way, with the two dead bodies in my head, like I'm an in-the-way monument to two little people from the red-light scene, and maybe I am.

Here comes Faller with a roguish but meaningful expression on his face.

'Iron Siggi,' he says.

'What?' I don't know what he's getting at.

'Iron Siggi,' he says again.

'What makes you suddenly come up with him? He's been retired for ages.'

'Well apparently he isn't,' says Faller. 'I've just been on the phone to him.'

I still don't understand.

'The phone number we picked up in the flat earlier,' he says. 'Do you remember the note you slipped me?'

'Yes, I remember,' I say. 'And?'

'I rang it and got through to Siggi. He says he's never even heard the name Margarete Sinkewicz. But obviously not a soul believes him. I'm about to go and have a heart-to-heart with him in person.'

'You're driving right over there?' I ask.

'What else,' he says. 'I'll bet he's waiting for me to swing by.'

He seems genuinely pleased to see his old acquaintance again. Iron Siggi, AKA Siegfried Eisele. Arrived in the Kiez from southern Germany in the early sixties, as what they used to call a talented young man: for a fiver, Siggi would do whatever needed doing. And then he took up boxing. His right hook soon got so dangerous that it earned him the nickname 'Iron', and soon, other people had to do the five-mark jobs. After three years, he owned a thriving brothel, right behind Hans-Albers-Platz – by Kiez standards the place was properly posh and the discreet atmosphere tended to draw in wealthy Hamburg society rather than tourists. And he was the boss of easily twenty lads who got their hands dirty for him, no matter what the job, because he paid very well and always made them feel that each of them could, one day, inherit his empire.

Not that it worked out like that. In the late eighties, the place got busted – there came a point when there was so much coke being done there that it wasn't nice anymore, you couldn't stand by and watch anymore, however much you loved the scene. There was a bit of a brouhaha among the elegant clientele, and certain people lost their high offices. Iron Siggi got almost ten years for procurement, grievous bodily harm, blackmail and organised crime. A lot of his boys went down too. Faller maintains that Siggi Eisele had legions of men beaten to a pulp but never actually killed anybody.

I'm not so sure of that.

Once Siggi had done his time, we didn't hear much from him. He rented a nice little flat in the fancy Alster-side suburbs, lived off his private pension and attracted no further attention. Or so we thought.

I don't believe it. Iron Siggi, no way. He must be nuts.

'How about you?' asks Faller. 'Want to come along?'

'I'd rather get an early night for a change,' I say, 'my blood pressure's down in my boots somewhere. What's happening with the press conference?'

'Leaving it to the press officer,' he says. 'I'm busy.'

I watch him walk away. He's limping slightly, and as I know his hip sometimes twinges, and as I really don't deal well with him being in pain, it really ought to sting me, but as there's more than just a limp, as he's also whistling this funny little tune, I find myself grinning. Something seems to have woken him right up again.

My phone rings.

Carla.

'Hey,' I say.

She's crying.

'What's the matter?' I ask.

Please, no more problems today.

'Hold on, I'll just step outside, OK?'

Sobbing. Outside, it's getting dark.

'Is this about Fernando?'

Her crying intensifies, so I take that as a yes.

'Where are you?' I ask.

Tears.

'In the café?'

Nothing.

'Outside my front door?'

'Yes.'

A very small voice. Carla will go and stand outside my door anytime she's in a bad way, day or night, regardless of whether or not I'm likely to be at home.

'Don't move then. I'll be there in five minutes, OK?'

'OK.'

'See you soon,' I say.

'Don't hang up,' she says, her voice stifled.

'OK,' I say, 'but the less I talk, the faster I'll be.'

'OK,' she says.

'I'll set off now then, and you just stay there, OK?'

'Mm-hm,' she says, and doesn't make another peep, like a good girl, even tries to suppress her sobs, while I run as fast as I can over crossings and streets.

I don't want to leave her alone a minute longer than necessary.

The cautious spring sun hasn't quite departed, there's still a little light, and I can already see Carla outside my building. She's wearing a grey coat that's way too big for her. I bet she's only got a skimpy little dress on under it. Her long, dark hair is down, her curls are untidy, her shoulders droop. She's got her phone to her ear and can probably hear me breathing.

Now she lifts her head and looks at me.

Her eyes have no sparkle at all, I've never seen her like that, and her mascara has cascaded down her cheeks. They're all black so it takes a moment for me to see the blue bruise shimmering around her left eye. I can't believe it. Fernando, you arsehole.

Once I finally reach her, I'm so out of breath I can't speak. We look at each other, still holding our phones to our ears. The tears are welling out of her eyes again. I take her phone from her and snap it shut, then I shut mine up and hold her in my arms. She's trembling.

'He hit you,' I say.

She shakes her head.

'Now, don't tell me you walked into a door.'

'No,' she says, pulling away from me. 'No, yes, well, no, it wasn't like that.' She wipes her coat sleeve over her face. Now it's seriously smeary.

'Can we get shit-faced first?' she asks.

'Fine by me,' I say.

Always fine by me.

WELL-HIDDEN BEAUTY

We're the first people there, so we've got plenty of time to take care of Carla's face. She ran out of her café with nothing, just her phone and not even a key, but her regular, the one who's always there and whose coat she nicked, will sort it out. He knows the ropes and could run the joint by himself if need be. And he knows that Carla loses the plot now and then.

He's probably secretly in love with her.

She's sitting in front of me in her see-through dress, her bare feet in strappy stilettos, the coat around her shoulders. She's stopped shivering. The pub is small and bathed in soft, yellow light. If you sit at the bar and look out, you can spend the whole evening watching a rather unspectacular square with a well-hidden beauty, which only reveals itself once you've spent a few weeks staring at it. I've spent whole nights just looking at the square. I know it inside and out, in spring, in summer, in autumn and in winter. Its beauty is indescribable. There's something emotional about it. It seems to respect and to love the people who cross it, to take care of them and to watch their backs, it just seems to have a big heart.

But perhaps you have to have experienced it for yourself.

The best thing about this place, however, is undoubtedly the barman. He has north-Indian roots but speaks with a Swabian accent, and has a side-line as a cycle courier. He mixes sharp little cocktails in shot glasses and only speaks when he has something important to say. The bar he stands behind is so small that he keeps having to wrestle the DJ for the scrap of space. They keep squeezing past each other but in a nice kind of way.

I order two double vodkas and a wet napkin. Carla downs her vodka and immediately orders another while I cautiously dab her face. She winces a little as I approach the black eye, but all in all, we put her back together pretty OK.

'So,' I say, downing my vodka too. 'Tell me.'

'Well,' she says. 'I saw him this afternoon, from a distance, he was walking down the road and I was on my way back from the cash-and-carry. He was with a woman, had her on his arm. I thought, uh-huh, who knows, could be his cousin or something, I'm such an idiot. But then the woman turned sideways and I saw her belly. She was pregnant. Pregnant, you know? I thought I was going mad.'

I take a breath and wonder if I should say anything, but Carla continues: 'I wanted to play it cool and not freak out and stay calm and wait and see what happened, I thought there might be an explanation, it might all work out, but then he turns up in the café like he doesn't have a care in the world, kisses me on the throat, and so I ask him what's going on and who that woman was, and then he comes out and says he's sorry, he'd wanted to break it to me gently, GENTLY, he says, but she's his fiancée. Fiancée, he says? FIANCÉE!'

She necks her second double vodka and orders a third.

'Oh, wow,' I say.

'Fucking arsehole. The woman's six months gone. In the last six months, we've split up and got back together again three times. So then I did flip, and I socked him one.'

'Slapped his face?' I ask.

'No,' she says, and takes a huge swig. 'A straight right to the chin.'

Holy shit. Carla's as strong as an ox in the arms from heaving crates of drink around. I guess Fernando hit the deck in front of a room full of people, and that will have seriously embarrassed him.

'You knocked him down?'

She nods.

'And then he hit back,' I say.

She nods again, and for a moment she looks pretty satisfied.

'What now?' I ask.

'He can kiss my arse,' she says, 'but this time forever.' She downs her third vodka, puts the glass on the bar, and her top lip starts to tremble, uh-oh, she'll be crying again in a moment. I hurriedly order more drinks, and swig. Carla's drinking at twice my rate, and that's saying something. Plus we're smoking like the devil. The music in the pub's getting louder, the light's getting darker, the fog's getting thicker.

'What's going on here, then?'

Way too suddenly, Klatsche is standing behind us, or rather between us, he's got his arms around us both. Carla tries to look at him but it's not working too well, her eyes keep slipping away.

'We've got ... something to ... celebrate,' she says.

'Must be something pretty special,' he says.

'Exactly,' she says. 'Fernando's a ... stupid arse ... end of.'

Klatsche pulls a face, orders a beer and gestures that he's going to make himself scarce, that he'll be in another corner of the bar for a while. I nod. But when his beer arrives, Carla can't go on. She slips off her stool, right into Klatsche's arms. It's a really funny sight, him standing there with a beer in one hand and Carla in the other.

'Er, yeah,' he says.

I can't help laughing, and my cigarette drops out of my hand.

'OK, chickens,' he says, 'listen up. Uncle Klatsche's going to take Carla home now and get her off to bed, and Auntie Chas can stay here while I'm gone, drink a glass of water now and then, and keep a firm eye on my beer.'

'Carla hasn't got her key on her,' I say.

'Then I'll put her in my bed,' he says.

'Perfect,' I say, thinking: and then you can come and sleep with me, ha-ha.

Klatsche orders me a water and throws Carla over his left shoulder. He literally throws her over his shoulder. I watch him. Man, I like that guy. I drink a bit of my water, start waiting for him to come back, and doodle on the beermat that's right under my nose.

BEHIND THE CLOUDS, THE STARS ARE DOING THEIR THING

'Zandvoort?'

Klatsche.

I didn't even see him come in.

'Who's that?'

'No one,' I say, crossing out the name.

Klatsche sits beside me at the bar. He gulps down his beer, which is duly still sitting there. I order two more.

'Is Carla OK?'

'She's in my bed,' he says. 'She's had such a skinful she'll sleep until at least tomorrow lunchtime. Whose coat is she wearing?'

'Oh,' I say, 'don't worry about it.'

The barman puts down our two beers.

'Klatsche,' I say, 'do you remember Iron Siggi?'

'Sure,' he says. 'One of the Kiez greats!' His eyes glint a little. 'Shame the old boy retired.'

'Can you imagine a guy like him ever coming out of retirement?'

'Anytime,' he says. 'Just as soon as there is anything to interest him. Why?'

'Just wondering,' I say.

He stares sidelong at me. Maybe I ought to copy Carla and just blow my own lights out. Klatsche slips closer to me but keeps his mouth ostentatiously shut. It's an international drinkers' agreement: don't talk at the bar unless absolutely necessary, but do sit close together. Doesn't work with everyone. But it works very well with Klatsche. We both have enough on our chests to talk into the dawn, there's the business with Basso yesterday, there's the business with us, there's life in general, but sometimes talking doesn't get you anywhere. Klatsche drains his beer, I drink mine and nod, he orders, and as the barman puts the bottles down, I budge a little closer over to him too, and a second later, the liquor cabinet comes down.

The top glass shelf just collapses in on itself, taking two other shelves with it. And forty bottles of spirits. Boom. Like a bomb went off.

Then it's very quiet.

The shock makes the needle jump off the turntable.

'Fucking hell!' says the barman, very loudly and very sharply, but only once. He vanishes into a cubbyhole beside the toilets, fetches a broom and starts sweeping up the glass.

The rest of the bar looks as though someone paused the film. Nobody moves. That'll cost a lot of money, what just happened, everyone knows that. A good Saturday evening's takings just went down the drain, and all because the material was fatigued.

That's how it goes sometimes.

The guy next to Klatsche, who'd fallen asleep with his head on the bar, wakes up and starts, very gently, to stir.

'Man,' he says, while everyone else is still holding their breath. 'Man, it stinks like a brewery in here.'

Now the DJ slowly regains his composure, puts a new record on, people pluck up their courage, start to move a tiny bit, talk quietly away to themselves and carry on drinking. The barman gives a cautious smile.

I look over at Klatsche. He's trying to bite back a laugh and he'll burst any moment. I stand up and put money on the bar.

'Come on, baby,' I say, 'time to go.'

'Don't call me baby,' grins Klatsche.

I take his hand, God knows why. We walk out, the street is wet, it's started raining again. Somewhere behind the clouds, the stars are doing their thing and I know: this dirty little neck of the woods with its knackered cobblestones, dark houses, glittering strings of lights, its charm, its worries, its unimportant but endearing stories, its constant drizzle, this is my place. But I also know that I shouldn't try to hold on to things, because in the end, they'll always get lost.

Back at home, Klatsche unlocks the street door, we walk up the stairs, still holding hands, the old wooden staircase creaks under our feet, we hold each other tight up to the third floor, we stop outside our flats. Mine is on the left, his on the right. The way a hand feels when you just hold it. And forget everything attached to it for a moment. It's dark in the stairwell, the light's broken, isn't it. I can't see his face, but it's so close to me I can feel it. His cheeks are wet with rain.

My drunken friend is occupying his bed and he doesn't even have a couch. I should take him in, just for friendship's sake. If I don't take him in, he'll have to sleep on the floor tonight. We're standing in this shitty stairwell, face to face.

'Klatsche,' I say.

'Yes?'

'What's your name?'

'Can't remember,' he says.

'Please,' I say. 'I really want to know your actual name.'

I need to know. I want to hold on to it, I'll write it down and then I'll put the paper in the bottommost drawer and forget it. Because it'll be like nothing happened, but I'll know that something happened.

His face comes even closer, his lips are somewhere between the back of my neck and my hair and it's not easy to hold out.

'Henri,' he says.

'Henri?' I say.

'Correct.'

OK, Henri. Then let's see what else we can start tonight.

So young so young
you really shouldn't be
going around like that
unprotected
you really shouldn't
I didn't tell her so
it's not my place
but I saw
and I helped her
and I think she wanted
to get to the sea
and then I sat
with her a while
and told her
what it was like for me
that day
when I got so scared
and she listened to me

WALKING IS KIND OF TOUGH

There's a tank parked on my head. Some large, heavy, metal object, and the thing's ringing like mad, and it must have been going on a while because Klatsche's slapping a flat hand in the direction the ringing's coming from, narrowly missing my head.

Klatsche?

Oh no.

That's not good.

That's not good at all.

He oughtn't to be lying beside me. Least of all with no clothes on.

I get my hands on the ringing monster, oh – it's my phone. I open my eyes, it's bright, very bright, far too bright, I grab a sheet, wrap myself up in it and make it to the window, it's freezing in here, who opened the big window, and where did it even come from anyway? Has it always been here?

Klatsche growls something and turns over.

'Hello?'

'Calabretta here.'

'What time is it?'

'Nearly nine, boss.'

'Am I on duty?'

'You always say you're always on duty.'

My heart is hammering, my head is clattering. I'm trying to get my eyes under control.

'What's happened?'

'We've got the next body.'

I come over dizzy.

'Wig?'

'Wig.'

I have to hold on to the nearest wall.

'Where?'

'At the port,' he says, 'between the Fish Auction Hall and the big furniture store. Behind one of those fancy restaurants, the Riviera.'

'I'll be there in fifteen minutes.'

I hang up, pull the sheet around my shoulders and glance at Klatsche. He's lying on his belly, his left arm stretched down beside him. I can see him breathing, see him sleeping deeply. Oh God, I wish I could lie back down with him, turn back time a couple of hours and then stop and end of story.

Holy shit.

I give the bed a wide berth, creep into the bathroom, brush my teeth, avoid looking in the harsh mirror, and I'm out of there. The sun is feigning nice weather, but it's pretty feeble, it can't manage to pump any colour into the early-morning Kiez. The terraces around these parts are as grey as my face. There are a few people hanging around in corners: they went astray, the night swallowed them up and then spat them back out again, and now they seem to have forgotten what they were wanting and where they belong.

The asphalt under my boots is sending little jolts through my knee up into my head. Walking is kind of tough. I hail a taxi and let it take me to the Riviera, out on the streets, my world passes by on a Friday morning. Somehow, it used to be a bit livelier.

The Riviera is on probably one of the most expensive stretches of the Elbe bank. Here, Hamburg is Hanseatic, chic, urbane, barely a kilometre from the Reeperbahn. Before I get out of the taxi, I take a deep breath in and out again, tie up my hair and try, as best as I can, to get ready for the sight of a dead woman.

RIVIERA

Everything looks like it's under a dome, the tall brick buildings, the docks over the river, the Elbe lying motionless in between, the gulls, hovering in the air, seeming barely to move. As if it's all just a backdrop, the first glimpse of a nasty story that's beginning here.

I can see Faller from way off. Crumpled coat, hat askew, arms hanging. He looks knackered. He's saying exactly the right thing, of course. The undertaker's lads are leaning against their hearse, offering a discreet hello, preferring not to stand out. I get the feeling that I'm creeping past them in slow motion, or at least as if I weren't even here. As if I were one of the gulls in the sky. I can still feel Klatsche's hand on my hip and I push it away.

'*Moin*,' says a uniformed officer, touching his hat with his index finger.

He's young and rather pale around the nose. If I were in a better state, I'd smile at him, lay my hand on his shoulder and tell him that not everything in this job is as bad as this here, this morning, and that even I sometimes look quite decent. But I'm not in anything remotely approaching that kind of state. I just nod to him briefly.

Faller turns around.

He can always hear who's behind him, he recognises people by their step. There are a few deep furrows around his mouth, his face is impressively grey, and when the body comes into view behind him, I immediately understand why. Somehow I'd had the naïve hope that this might still be a drug-related death, that the guys might have got mixed up somehow. But it's exactly as written in Faller's face: our killer is going into serial production, playing by all the rules of that ugly artform. It's going to be bad.

The girl is sitting on a director's chair, the chair's leaning against the back of the Riviera, which towers arrogantly into the sky, the girl's eyes are open and looking at the water. She's younger than Margarete Sinkewicz, she's rather short and very thin, she's no more than nineteen but has the body of a fourteen-year-old, translucent skin with no body hair of any kind. And then ... well. This time, the wig is platinum blonde, Hollywood curls, shoulder length. There's dried blood stuck to the girl's brow. Everyone present knows what's hidden under that wig, but nobody's talking about it. All in all, it wouldn't surprise me if they've all lost the power of speech.

I can't hold it back, it happens too fast.

''Scuse me,' I say, gripping Faller tight, and throw up behind his back onto the cobbles. Great.

Madam Prosecutor is on top form and has started by puking all over the crime scene.

'Morning, boss,' says Faller.

I wipe my mouth and gather up the remains of my face.

'Sorry,' I say again.

'That's OK,' says Faller, 'I've been there.'

I try for a smile.

'Who found her?'

Faller nods to the right. There's an old man standing there, holding a fishing rod and crying.

'Calabretta just went for coffee,' says Faller. 'Shall I call him and ask him to bring another?'

I try the smile thing again, shake my head, squeeze Faller's forearm and walk over to the old man. Which means passing the dead girl. The closer you get to her, the daintier she looks. Her skin looks like a thin layer of snow. It's cynical, but perhaps what makes the sight of her even sadder than that of the silicone-enhanced, solarium-tanned Margarete is not just the fact that she's the second body but, above all, that this girl looks so untouched by life; she looks like a doll.

Her eyes staring at the water, the trickle of blood on her forehead, something about it all resembles a smashed-up idea. As if someone has shattered something truly delicate. I feel sick again, I have to take a little break and cling on to the railing for a moment, the one that's here to protect people from tipping into the Elbe.

Once I can stand up straight again, I try to get as close as possible to the old man without touching him or in any way crowding him. He's crying quietly to himself.

'I'm Chastity Riley,' I say, 'state prosecutor.'

He doesn't stir, and the hand that's gripping his fishing rod is almost white.

'This must have been a nasty shock for you, sir,' I say.

'She's sitting on my chair,' he says, shutting his eyes. 'If I didn't keep leaving it standing around here, she wouldn't be sitting there like that. My wife keeps telling me I oughtn't to leave the chair standing around.'

His shoulders start to twitch. He's crying like a child. He's at least eighty.

'Do you come here every morning?' I ask.

He nods.

'What do you fish for?'

'Zander,' he says. 'I don't have a fishing licence.'

He looks at me for a brief moment. His eyes are a hazy aqua blue, maybe they used to look like Paul Newman's.

'Don't worry,' I say, 'that's not my department. You fish as much as you like.'

'I'm not coming here again,' he says, wiping the tears from his parchment skin with his free hand.

'What time do you come out?'

'Half past six, or thereabouts,' he says.

'This morning too?'

'It was just after six. And there she was, sitting on my chair.'

His voice breaks, then chokes.

'Did you see anybody?'

He shakes his head and starts to cry more heftily again. I put my hand on his shoulder and hope he'll have the time to forget this morning. Then I press my card into his hand.

'Know what,' I say. 'Call me when you've found a new spot. I'd like to come along.'

The old man smiles at me through his tears and slips the card into his anorak.

I have no idea how to get back past the girl without fainting.

JETTIES

Later, once the dead girl's on her way to pathology, we walk a few paces, Faller and me. Faller's got his hands in his coat pockets and isn't coming out with anything, but I know there's something the matter.

'What?' I ask.

'Hm,' he says.

I offer him a cigarette. He declines.

'What?' I ask again.

'I did go to see Iron Siggi yesterday,' he says.

Siggi. Oh yeah.

'Oh yeah,' I say. 'How is he?'

'He was in a funny mood,' says Faller, 'wasn't pleased to see me.'

'Faller,' I say, 'you got him put away back then.'

'Bah,' he says, 'that's old news. That's all in the past.'

If I were Siggi I wouldn't see it that way, but whatever.

'He was totally distant,' he says, 'as if he hadn't even noticed that I was there.'

'Faller,' I say, 'we've got two young women dead in the space of a few days. Is Iron Siggi really that important?'

'I think so,' says Faller. 'After all, our first victim had his phone number.'

'OK,' I say, 'but what does the psychological state of some old crook have to do with us?'

'Trust me, Chas. I think it's got a lot to do with us.'

We walk along the waterfront a bit further, not speaking. I'm slowly coming round. And somewhere between jetties six and seven, Faller holds his arm out to me and I link up with him.

'You ought to clean your boots, you know,' he says. 'They look a state.'

TOUGH NUT TO CRACK

I almost managed to persuade Faller to come with me to Carla's. He's never been to her place, and I thought, after a morning like that, it would do him good to let a little of her nature rub off on him. But he preferred to go home for lunch, wanted to see his wife.

Quite right.

If you have a home, you ought to go there.

I pull the café door open, a little too roughly I think, and I feel like an idiot. To get rid of the feeling, I slip off my boots like I'm coming in from filthy weather. Zandvoort is sitting at a table by the wall. He nods as our eyes meet. Carla isn't there, and standing behind the counter is the nice regular customer whose coat she borrowed yesterday. He looks a bit out of his depth but is doing quite well. The place is full and the clientele seem content.

'Where's Carla?' I ask, slipping onto a barstool.

He shrugs his shoulders; his pale hair is standing bolt upright, snapping to attention.

'No idea,' he says, frowning, 'not here, anyway.'

'Maybe she's still sleeping it off,' I say.

'I see,' he says. 'Do you happen to know where my coat is?'

'Safe.'

He nods, rinses a few glasses and enquires, more of himself than of me: 'Why am I even doing this?'

Because you've got the hots for her, pumpkin, I think.

I can feel Zandvoort's eyes on the back of my neck.

And what am I even doing here?

A diversionary tactic.

I'm an idiot.

I lift my chin, straighten up, turn around and head towards Zandvoort. Carla always says I need to learn how to approach men. Here you go, I think. Zandvoort twitches the left-hand corner of his mouth up a bit, it's not a proper smile, more of an 'I knew it'.

I feel like a lump of prey.

He feels to me like a predator at a notorious watering hole. One where the animals always tell each other: don't go there, no matter how beautiful the light is on the water. You *know* the lions lie in wait there.

So actually, not a good type to practise on.

The lion gets up.

He wants to take my coat before I sit down.

'Thanks,' I say, 'but I'll keep it on.'

Only a little cover, but better than nothing.

'How are you?' he asks.

'Work's giving me a little bother,' I say. Dammit, that's none of his business.

'What do you do for a living, then?' he asks. 'I don't know anything about you, except that you seem to like wearing that funny trench coat.'

As if Carla hasn't painted him the most dazzlingly colour-ful picture of how I earn my crust. So please.

'State prosecutor,' I say.

He pulls an impressed face. 'So? An exciting new case or just the usual tax evasion?'

He really does think he's the greatest.

'I can't talk about ongoing investigations.'

I look him in the eyes. Steel grey, I wasn't wrong the first time. I like the way he wears his hair, just combed back like that. Not something you see so often nowadays. Today he's not wearing a suit but black trousers and a grey roll-neck. In other respects, he's even cagier than me. No wonder Carla thinks he might suit me. I notice that he's studying me too, and suddenly I feel badly dressed and unshowered. I'm wearing yesterday's white shirt and old jeans. I hope there are no puke stains anywhere. I squint down at myself and can't see any.

'Got any plans for this evening?' he asks.

'I never have any plans for the evening,' I say, 'unless there's football on.'

'What's your team?' he asks.

'Sankt Pauli,' I say. 'How about you?'

'Alemannia Aachen,' he says, 'not easy either.'

I have to grin.

'Would you have dinner with me tonight?'

No.

'Sorry,' I say, 'I'm afraid I can't.'

'Why not?'

You're kind of creepy. And I don't want to get tangled up.

'Diet,' I say.

'Oh, please,' he says. 'Nobody's buying that. With your figure.'

Slimeball.

'How about a glass of wine?'

'I'd love one,' I say, 'but right now.'

He smiles, shakes his head.

'You really are a tough nut to crack.'

He goes over to the bar and orders two glasses of Chardonnay from the nice regular, who is doing an excellent job there.

'Well, I won't see you this evening then,' Zandvoort says when he comes back with my wine.

'No,' I say.

'So, when will we meet again?'

'I'll probably be here Monday lunchtime.'

'I'll make that work,' he says.

In a funny way, I get the feeling that this is the exact moment when he starts to step on my toes.

INFECTIOUS

A glass of wine is practically medicinal: I'm doing brilliantly. I can hardly remember this morning's hangover, and even the dead girl seems an unpleasant and wrong, but now distant, memory. I feel almost like a normal human being. I walk past the landing bridges towards the taxi rank, need to get to Eppendorf, to pathology. Obviously, I don't particularly want to go to pathology, not again, but I have to. And at least my new friend Betty Kirschtein might be there, maybe.

There's not much happening on the water so I see the guy at once. He's sitting on one of those heavy, cast-iron bollards that you fasten the ropes of ships at anchor to. He's looking out over the water, he's very thin, his skin is pale and his short, soft hair is the colour of roebuck. He turns his head towards me and looks at me. There's quite a large birthmark right over his upper lip, which gives his face a very special clarity.

The clatter of my heels seems to disturb his thoughts, but he doesn't look away again the way people normally do. He looks me in the eyes as I walk closer. When I'm level with him, I can't just walk on. I stop because I have to. I stand there, right by the water, looking at this young stranger. The situation is peculiar, I ought to say something to make it better, but my throat feels laced up, I can't utter a sound, and his gaze pushes under my skin like a cold finger. I don't know how long we're caught in this disembodied embrace, I'm not sure exactly what this is, but it's powerful. And the longer I look him in the eyes, the more its nature appears: a pain, so overflowing as to be infectious.

I gather all my strength and actually manage to unclench my teeth.

'Can I help you?'

He twitches, casts his eyes back down, turns his head away and looks back at the water.

'Go away,' he says. So quietly I can barely hear it.

'But...'

'Go away,' he says, loudly this time, he hurls it in my direction, without looking at me again.

'Just go.'

Once I'm sitting in the taxi, I give myself a slap on each cheek so that I can regain a grip.

WILL YOU PLEASE DO THE PARENTAL STUFF?

Everything on the pathology stairs is the same as ever. The disinfectant gets into my nose, the prevailing cold of the cellar is beckoning to me, even from this distance and, when I see that Faller and the doctor aren't alone, my heart sinks to where it likes to be: in my boots. Faller is talking to a woman in an elegant, cream-coloured spring coat, who is sitting on a chair, sunk down beside the wash basin. The doc is standing woodenly in front of the slab with the body, beside him is a man who has his face buried in his hands. They look like two people who have just lost everything. Relatives. Relatives are even worse than corpses. Relatives are in the thick of things. Help.

Betty Kirschtein isn't there. Faller sees me, puts his hand on the woman's shoulder for a moment and comes over to me.

'The parents?' I ask.

'They just identified the girl,' he says. 'She just turned nineteen.'

'And might have danced in a strip club?'

'The parents don't know about anything like that,' he says.

'What was her name?' I ask.

'Henriette Auer,' Faller whispers, but the mother hears her daughter's name anyway and lobs me a glance that blames me for everything.

'Will you do the parental stuff, please, Faller?'

I can't, not today.

Faller nods.

'Does the doc know anything yet?' I ask.

'He hasn't analysed the drug in her bloodstream yet, but he's working on the assumption that it's the same stuff he found in Margarete Sinkewicz.'

'Anything else?'

'Same games as last time,' he says. 'She was throttled with a cable tie, no self-defence, then she was undressed, scalped and taken to the Elbe. The whole thing happened between one and three in the morning.'

'He's going to kill more women, isn't he?'

Faller bites his lips.

The girl's mother is still staring at me. It's hard to bear a look like that.

'See you tomorrow in the team meeting, OK?'

Faller nods.

'I'll talk to the press,' he says, 'and try to persuade them to keep stumm until Monday. If we don't get anything solid soon, that's going to get tricky.'

I make another attempt at getting my face under control.

'OK,' I say. 'Later on, I'll show a picture of Henriette around the dance club where Margarete worked. I might find something out there.'

'Should I come along?' Faller asks.

'Do you want to come?'

'I wouldn't say *want* to,' he says, 'but somehow I get the feeling that you oughtn't go alone today, however much you normally like it that way.'

'You don't have to come into the Kiez if you don't want to, Faller. I'll take Calabretta with me if that makes you feel better.'

He takes my hand, gives it a squeeze and says: 'See you tomorrow, in your office.'

I smile at him, he turns away, goes back to Henriette Auer's mother and takes her hand too, and I'm extraordinarily grateful to him for that and, in return, I try to clear the last traces of the memory of the boy from the jetties from my head.

TEXTBOOK COP

Nothing beats a good relationship with the press. Patschinski and the other reporters have promised not to publish any stories about the second death until Monday. So long as we don't stint on information thereafter. I can live with that.

'Guess you just need the pressure,' Patschinski said on the phone.

'Pressure,' I said, 'is absolutely the last thing I need right now, but I'll happily talk to you about it again on Monday.'

I take Calabretta with me to the Acapulco. He can do a dangerous look and, all in all, he's exactly the man for a late-night visit to the red-light district. When we get out of his car at the Davidwache, the dusk is creeping down over the horizon. In my coat pocket I've got a polaroid of Henriette. If it weren't for that trace of blood on her brow, you could think she was sleeping. There's something unsettlingly peaceful about the photo.

We walk down the Reeperbahn and turn onto the Grosse Freiheit. Here and there, neon signs flash, advertising booze, sex and striptease. And the retired pimps, who now work as touts supposed to lure the clientele into the establishments, are already loitering about a bit on the street, putting on their sea-captain looks.

The red-light district is warming up.

The Acapulco's relatively near the top of the Freiheit. Hanging over the entrance is an old-fashioned neon sign in garish colours, touting their girls. The lights are still out. As if the place was in mourning.

Calabretta opens the door, glances around and then he says: 'OK. Come on in.'

He always does that, probably even off duty, even when he goes for breakfast with a sweetheart. Watched too many films, I reckon.

The room is dark, all the lamps are off, except for a weak yet cold lightbulb over the stage. An older woman in a smock is just taking the chairs off the tables. Dancing on the pole on the stage is a girl in pink underwear. The man she's dancing for is slumped deep in his chair in the front row, you can only see him from behind. Black, glossy hair, black leather jacket.

'*Moin*, sir,' says Calabretta.

The man turns his head and narrows his eyes, the girl stops dancing. He turns back to her.

'Carry on.'

Then he stands up and comes towards us.

'Can I help you?'

'Vito Calabretta, Hamburg CID,' says Calabretta, 'and this is Chastity Riley, State Prosecution Service.'

The guy nods, we nod back.

'So,' he says, 'if you're here about Maggie, you lot have already been around. I've got nothing to blame myself for.'

'Is that Maggie's replacement, dancing there?' I ask, nodding in the direction of the girl on the pole.

He looks me firmly in the eyes and doesn't answer.

'What can I do for you?' he asks. His left incisor is broken.

Calabretta holds the photo of Henriette under his nose.

'Know her?'

He takes the picture from him and pins it down on a table.

'Henny.'

'An angler found her beside the Elbe this morning,' I say.

'Did the girl work here?' Calabretta asks.

The guy nods and stares at the picture.

'My God,' he says, 'she was so young.'

'How long had she been with you?' I ask.

'Two weeks,' he says. 'Had her first proper performance yesterday. Really talented on the pole.'

'She ought to have been studying for her exams, not cavorting about on your stage,' says Calabretta.

'I pay well,' says the guy, 'and if a girl likes fancy handbags, why shouldn't she dance for them...'

'Did you see if Henriette left the club with anyone?' asks Calabretta.

'She left alone, just after one-thirty.'

'Did she have any friends here?' I ask.

'My girls all get on well enough, but I can't tell you who's friends with who. Their private affairs are none of my business.'

'Can we speak to the girls?'

Calabretta's going for determined and tight-lipped. He really is a textbook cop, you have to give him that. And he always wears his jackets too tight so that there's no mistaking the gun beneath them.

'The first show's at eight, so the girls get here around seven,' says the guy.

'Will you take care of it?' I ask Calabretta.

'Sure,' he says. 'I'd better just stay here.'

The leather-jacket guy claps him jovially on the shoulder and glances at the dancing girl.

'No problem, man.'

Oh no, fraternisation ahoy.

'Er, Calabretta?' I say. 'Would you bring a female colleague along too? The girls will need a sympathetic face to look into when they learn that two of their number are now dead.'

THE SIGNS ARE LIT UP ALL NIGHT LONG

It's now evening in Sankt Pauli, it's Friday, the mile is filling up and starting to glitter. The suburban youth has glammed itself up and pre-loaded at home, now it's descending upon the pubs and clubs of the Grosse Freiheit. The thirty-year-olds are strolling through the bars and having a few drinks before heading out to little club shows. The pensioners are on their way to the operetta house, where they'll subject themselves to a musical, but first they'll have a squint at the sex shops for a giggle. I get myself off home.

Walk down the Grosse Freiheit – its lower section is a world away from the hustle and bustle at the other end. There's not much here apart from two legendary music venues – this end of the street practically exudes tranquillity. On the corner with Paul-Roosen-Strasse, there's another noisy spit-and-sawdust pub, opposite which a new place is trying to look respectable, and then you turn the corner and it's a residential area. A bakery, a supermarket, the greengrocer, the hairdresser. If I turn left at the deli, I'm on my road. Leon, the northern-English guy, is standing behind his bar in the Bar Centrale, he waves to me and I wave back, I walk past the takeaway fish shop, outside which a group of teenage girls are smoking cigarettes, next to them, the cycle couriers are standing outside their workshop, where you can buy the fastest bikes in town. The Kandie Shop is already shut, but the sign advertising good coffee is lit up all night long, and right at the bottom, at the end of the street, Achmed is just closing up his kiosk. The kebab shop next door is opening up, ready to take over. From now on, the beer's sold there.

I really want to talk to Carla. I pull my phone out of my coat pocket and dial her number. She doesn't answer. I call the café. Nobody answers there either. The nice regular seems to have given up. My God, she can't still be comatose, last night wasn't as bad as all that.

Sheesh, *I've* been standing to attention all day.

She's got some nerve. I really would like to speak to her. I look for my key and stick it in the lock.

'Hey.'

Oh. Klatsche.

'Hey,' I say.

I almost slam the front door in his face.

'Where've you been?' he asks.

I don't know what to answer, there's so much I could say and it's so hard for me to say anything at all.

'Where are you going?' I ask.

'On call,' he says, raising his right eyebrow and swinging his toolbox. 'Let me through, I'm the locksmith.'

I laugh, but it's a bit exaggerated, the joke wasn't that good. If it was one.

'Have you only just woken up?' I ask.

He puts on a crumpled grin and says: 'It was a stormy voyage yesterday.'

I glance at my feet and then look back into his eyes.

Phew.

'Is Carla awake?'

'Well, she won't have gone home asleep.'

'She's not at yours?'

'Nu-uh,' he says. 'When I got back to my flat an hour ago the bed was empty. Why?'

'She's not at the café and she's not answering her phone.'

'Are you worried?'

'I always worry about Carla.'

'Ah,' he says, 'she's a big girl.'

She's not, I think.

'Hey,' he says, and kisses my forehead.

Yikes.

'Your friend can look after herself. I'll call you later, OK, I've got to go.'

'OK,' I say, and he's gone, and I'd been meaning to say, nah, don't worry, you don't have to, and now I'm watching as he strolls down the road and unlocks the Volvo, and before he gets in, he turns back and waves to me, and it would have been way cooler if I hadn't been standing here staring after him.

I go in and drag myself up the stairs, shit, today's left a serious dent in me.

As I go to put my key in the keyhole, the door swings open.

Klatsche's such an idiot, opens doors for a living but is clearly incapable of closing them now and then.

I turn on the hall light and shut the door behind me. Something's not right. It smells of aftershave. Klatsche doesn't, he smells of lock oil and soap. I walk into the living room, switch on the light and look around. Everything seems the same as ever. Brown sofa, bare, super-dirty floorboards, no curtains, a TV, a minibar, the desk. I look in the kitchen and the bedroom. Klatsche actually made the bed.

I go back to the living room. It's here. Something isn't right here. My desk is looking at me. It looks like it wants to tell me something. When I pull open the drawer, I feel dizzy. My gun is gone. Somebody was in my flat and they've taken my gun.

I keel over on the spot.

IN THE FUCKING DOORFRAME

It's nearly midnight, I'm lying on the floor and staring at the ceiling. In the last two hours, I've called Carla ten times, and ten times she hasn't answered her phone. The staring-at-the-ceiling is an attempt at calming down, but it's not working.

There's a knock at the door. I hold my breath. There's another knock. I stand up, wipe down my jeans, walk to the door and open it.

'Hey,' says Klatsche.

'Hey,' I say, thinking: nice to see you, things were so lonely just now.

Klatsche has a bottle of beer in each hand.

'Good idea?'

'Very good idea,' I say, sliding down the doorframe and making myself comfortable there. Klatsche follows suit, pulls his lighter from his trouser pocket, opens the beers and gives me one.

'Thanks,' I say, interlinking my legs with his.

'OK like this?' he asks.

'Great,' I say. 'Do you happen to have a couple of cigarettes on you too?'

He fishes in his jacket pocket and pulls out a crumpled soft pack of Luckies, unfiltered. My hall lamp is throwing a nice, warm glow in his face. He looks a lot older than he did yesterday. He could easily pass for twenty-eight.

'Exactly four left,' he says, lighting one and posting it between my lips.

I draw in the smoke.

'The Kiez is freaking out,' he says.

'Friday evening, isn't it,' I say.

'I'm not an idiot,' he says. 'I know what happened. Everyone's talking about it.'

I take a sip of my beer.

'It was awful,' I say. 'The way she had been sat there, in that wig, looking at the water. She should have been finishing school in the summer.'

Klatsche lights himself a cigarette too. I drop a little ash on the floor.

'Wait a moment,' I say, 'I'll just get an ashtray.' From the living room, I ask: 'So what kind of stuff are people saying in the Kiez?'

'That there's a madman on the loose, mutilating dancers,' he says. 'They're all scared. There are some seriously big lads on the door of the Acapulco now, and none of the girls want to go anywhere alone. Some don't want to come to work anymore. One of the doormen at the casino says he saw a weirdo, at least six foot six, wearing a wig made of women's hair. But I think that's the start of an urban myth. You know how quick they start up round here.'

I slide down my side of the doorframe again and put the ashtray down in the stairway.

'Heard anything else about Basso?' I ask.

'Nah,' he says, 'everyone's keeping quiet. If a pimp gets killed it's always better not to say anything. The message is clear enough. It's just that the poor bloke had to die over it.'

'You liked him, huh?'

'Well, I hardly knew him. But the little fish have to stick together, right?'

He takes a swig of beer and drags on his cigarette.

'Have you got through to Carla yet?'

I shake my head.

'I'd rather not know where she is.'

'In the worst case,' he says, 'she's already dismembering Fernando.'

'Cut it out,' I say.

He laughs and, as if by accident, his left hand lands on my knee. I don't push it away, and I shut my eyes.

'Klatsche,' I say.

'Mm-hm,' he mumbles.

'Did you lock my door when you left?'

'Course,' he says, 'what d'you take me for?'

'The door was only on the latch,' I say.

'No,' he says.

'Yes,' I say, opening my eyes again.

Klatsche looks tired.

'Had someone been in your flat, baby?'

'It smelled of aftershave. Like someone from the Kiez had popped round for a visit.'

He takes a gulp of beer.

'Wow. Know what the visitor wanted?'

'I presume he wanted my gun,' I say. 'Because it's gone.'

'Didn't even know you had one.'

'I'm not meant to,' I say, taking another swig.

'What would a guy from the Kiez want with *your* gun?' he asks.

'To frighten me?'

'Who wants to frighten you? You're the fucking prosecution.'

'I've got no fucking idea, Klatsche.'

He strokes my knee a bit, again more as if by accident, and then we don't talk anymore, we drink up our beer after a fashion, each of us smokes a second cigarette and in the end we land up in two separate beds.

LEG IT

I convince myself that it's just going for a walk, just one of my usual walks to Carla's café. But it's not going for a walk. I'm scared and going at a bizarre clip. As if I were hoping that, with every metre I cover, the fear would shrink a little. But sadly, it doesn't work like that. The fear doesn't shrink. The fear grows the closer I get to my goal. I pass what used to be the harbour hospital, through the tatty woodland with its gnarly trees, walk down Venusberg, I sprint down the steps to the Portuguese Quarter and I'm scared. Just before I reach the café, the fear grows so huge that it's starting to lame me, it's like being trapped in a bad-dream world where you can't move your feet however hard you try, and I feel like the shops to my left and right, selling clothes and souvenirs, are laughing at me, like they find me being stuck to the asphalt too funny for words. When I rattle the café door and realise that it's locked, the fear turns to panic.

Carla's not there, the café's shut, she's never done that before. She always opens her café, no matter what. I try to calm my breathing and to make my blood pressure understand that it wouldn't help anyone if I fell over right at this moment. I call Carla's number but her phone's now switched off. I can hear a computerised voice on the line and a foghorn in the distance.

I kick the glass door, pound my fists against it, stick my forehead to it. I pull myself together and start running again; two streets over, I ring up a storm on Carla's doorbell. Nothing. I search my keyring for the slightly rusty key to her flat, which she once gave me, this one, this must be it. It fits. I race up the stairs and unlock her flat door, and the moment the door opens, I know, of course – Carla isn't here. In the sink there's a coffee cup with a rim of dried-on coffee at the bottom, everything else is perfectly neat and tidy. The bed's made, there's nothing lying around apart from one polka-dot dress hanging on the plush old armchair in the living room. The whole place looks as though the woman who lives here has just flown out on a weekend break. Carla can't have been here in the last two days. Since the Fernando shit came out. Fernando, that idiot. Maybe he knows where she is.

I double-lock Carla's flat, the way I always do at home – I'm constantly telling her that she should do the same, but she doesn't give a damn.

OK.

Down, out, leg it.

Fernando lives on the other side of the Michaeliskirche, behind the big publishing house, a monster of a workplace that inhales people every morning and spits them out again every evening, by which time they all look as though their blood has been pumped out over the course of the day, or at least as though their souls have been tampered with, and maybe that's true.

I cross the park below the church, it'll take me five minutes to get to Fernando's.

He opens up and stands, somewhat perplexed, in the doorframe, behind him in the kitchen is a dainty woman in a dressing gown. The woman is unmistakably pregnant.

'Come out,' I say.

'You want to beat me up too?' he asks.

The shiner on his left eye shimmers lilac and green.

'You'd deserve it,' I say.

He glares at me.

'Carla's gone,' I say.

'Oh,' he says, 'is she being dramatic again?'

'Watch it, or I'll get dramatic on you,' I say. 'Do you have any idea where she could be? Has she been in touch?'

'Wouldn't you rather come in?'

'Where the hell is Carla, Fernando?'

'Don't snarl at me like that, I haven't seen her since Thursday. And as far as I'm concerned, it can stay that way.'

'You're such an arsehole,' I say, and it does me the world of good to say so. Before I forget myself and do actually wallop him one, I turn on my heel and make myself scarce.

I'LL MAKE YOU A STAR

'What's the matter, boss?' Calabretta narrows his eyes. 'You look like a stale panettone. Maybe you ought to see a doctor.'

'I'm OK,' I say. 'I just slept badly.'

Hollerieth from forensics throws me an overbearing glance and strokes his moustache. Jackass. Schulle and Brückner are looking about as shit as me. I know they always get wrecked in the Kiez on a Friday evening – today, the two of them must have the hangover that I had yesterday. Brückner keeps scratching his head, Schulle can hardly peer out of his red eyes. Mr Borger is flicking through a football magazine.

'Going straight on to the match?' he asks me.

Oh, Lord. Today's the football. I'd totally forgotten.

'Dunno yet,' I say.

'But you can't leave your friend on her own in the stand,' he says. 'You do always go with a friend, don't you?'

'Yes, uh,' I say, 'my friend's not around.'

'Oh, where is she then?' asks Mr Borger, smiling at me.

'Don't know,' I say, 'I don't know where she is.'

Mr Borger furrows his brow and looks at me like I'm a

patient. He can smell it when people are all over the place. I act like I haven't noticed. My paranoia is really nobody's business here.

The door flies open, Faller comes in with Betty Kirschtein in his wake. It does me good to see them. Faller is freshly shaved and looks cheerful. Betty's had a haircut and her hair is now chin length. Not bad. Kind of, well, jaunty.

Faller takes off his hat and grips my shoulder for a moment in passing, then he sits down next to Calabretta, and Betty sits next to Faller, I smile at them both. Calabretta stands up and shakes hands with Betty, across Faller. He puts on his best smile and says: 'We haven't met. Vito Calabretta. CID.'

I see. He fancies her.

'Kirschtein,' she says, 'forensic medicine.'

Her voice again.

'So,' says Faller. 'Let's get started.'

Mr Borger puts his magazine away.

Schulle wipes his hand over his face, Brückner straightens his back, Hollerieth stares at me. What's his problem? One day, I think, one day we'll meet in some dark street. And then I'll sock you one.

'To sum up,' says Faller, 'we now have two young women dead. Both were dancers at the Acapulco. One was twenty-four, the other nineteen. Margarete Sinkewicz was a former cashier from Cottbus, Henriette Auer was still in year thirteen in Hamburg. As far as we know, the fact that they both danced at the same club was the only connection between them. Calabretta?'

'Margarete's friend Tatjana doesn't know much about Henriette and neither do the other girls at the Acapulco. She was apparently very reserved and, presumably because she didn't want anyone to know about her dancing, she didn't particularly want to socialise with the other dancers. They say they got the impression that Henriette primarily wanted to earn money and otherwise keep out of things. Margarete's death seems to have upset the girls more, somehow. She seems to have been an exceptionally kind person, often cooked for her colleagues, took care of them if someone wasn't feeling too well, or brought in presents. Her friend Tatjana says Maggie always took very good care of her and the other girls. Men, on the other hand, she always kept at a distance, didn't even have any admirers or anything.'

'But the way it looks,' I say, 'both girls went voluntarily with their killer. That really doesn't seem to fit, with Margarete in particular.'

Borger leans back and takes off his glasses.

'The man must have come across as entirely trustworthy,' he says. 'Or else it was someone from her past that nobody else knew about.'

'I don't believe that,' says Faller, 'if the chap was going after old acquaintances, there'd have to have been a link between Margarette and Henriette. And it doesn't look at all like there is. I think it was coincidence that these two girls in particular fell victim to him.'

'I think our man is just a smart chap,' says Mr Borger, 'who makes a good impression on young women.'

'Or one who has something to offer them,' I say.

'True,' says Borger. 'So what would that be, for a woman who is a pole dancer in a strip club? What could you tempt her with?'

'I'll make you a star,' says Betty Kirschtein.

'Exactly,' I say, 'that's sure to go down well.'

'I used to want to be a photographer,' says Brückner, 'so that I could say that very thing to all the pretty girls.'

'So, are we looking for a photographer?' I ask.

'Maybe,' says Mr Borger. 'Or someone in showbiz.'

'Has anyone spoken to Henriette Auer's friends yet?' asks Faller.

'We have,' says Schulle. 'They had no idea of Henriette's job. They thought she was going to dance classes. Which wasn't entirely wrong.'

'Did she have a boyfriend?' I ask.

'She was apparently popular with the boys, but didn't get involved with anyone,' says Schulle. 'Her friends say she was super ambitious and considered guys a waste of time.'

'So the whole "I'll make you a star" business would fit quite well,' says Borger.

'Doesn't sound so dumb to me either,' I say.

'What does the pathologist's report on Henriette say?'

'Basically the same as for Margarete,' says Betty Kirschtein. 'Our killer seems to have a really clear pattern. He served her up the same pills, phenobarbital, in the same way, with gin. Again, no sex and no signs of a fight, a cable tie again, some kind of carpet knife again, probably the very same one. But it almost looks like it didn't take him as long. As if he had a better idea what he was doing the second time around.'

'What do you make of it?' I ask Mr Borger.

'That could fit. Maybe he noticed that he finds this business easier than he thought he would. But if that's so, then something will have cracked, and we'll soon have a third victim. I'm afraid I have to put it like that. We don't have much time.'

Schulle rubs his face with his hands again, and now I do too.

'Anything else?' asks Faller.

'Yes,' says Hollerieth, clearing his throat. Everyone's looking at him and he's enjoying his moment. 'We've got footprints and a little DNA.'

'Hair?' I ask.

'Right,' says Hollerieth. 'This time we were in luck with the weather.'

'Are you sure they're his?' asks Calabretta.

'It was dry with hardly any wind yesterday morning,' says Hollerieth. 'No atmospheric conditions to mess things up for us. And there are a few short, pale-brown hairs on her throat and her upper body. I don't know whose else's they'd be, DI Calabretta.'

Show-off.

'Will the hair get us any further?' I ask.

'We know his hair colour at any rate,' says Faller. 'And we can look up his DNA on the computer. He might have cropped up somewhere before.'

'What shoe size is our man?' I ask.

'Forty-three, I'd say,' says Hollerieth.

'Which would put him at about five foot eleven,' says Betty.

'What does he do with the girls' clothes?' I ask, looking at Mr Borger.

'He keeps them,' says Mr Borger, 'I'm pretty certain of that. Just like their hair. And he has a special place for both.'

'Do we know anything particular about the wigs he's using?' I ask.

'We've traipsed round all the shops,' says Brückner. 'Hundreds of stage wigs like that are sold a day, they're bought by theatres, tourists and prostitutes alike, so it's hard to keep track of things. Unfortunately.'

'Is there any news on the dead pimp?' I ask.

'We're on it,' says Brückner. 'That Basso guy worked for anyone and everyone, regularly got mixed up with the worst of the lads out there, but in all his years, he never did manage to move up in the world. The Kiez keeps its mouth shut when we ask about him. It's possible the business is entirely unrelated to our case and it only looks superficially like they're linked. Basso was constantly in trouble. I'll try to get on to our sources. Maybe they can help.'

'OK,' I say. I can't help thinking about Carla, and I look at my phone. Nothing. 'Anything else?'

General looking around the room and headshaking. Hollerieth has already stood and is packing up his stuff.

I go out onto the balcony for another smoke with Betty,

she eats another apple, Calabretta watches her cautiously from a distance, Faller comes for a smoke with us too, and then I head off to the match.

SCOTT AND JAMES

Heavy clouds are hanging over the Millerntor Stadium. I reckon it's going to rain tonight. I've bought more cigarettes, I'm standing in our regular spot on the south stand, watching the boys warm up and acting like nothing's going on. I haven't been at a match without Carla for ages. My old acquaintance, the benefits guy, isn't here yet either. Is everyone dumping me tonight, or what?

Once, I went to the Waldstadion in Frankfurt with my dad, and got lost. I was eight or nine. It was an exciting day. Eintracht were playing Bayern, all of Frankfurt was beside itself. My dad and I were standing down by the fence so that I could see better. I was hot, I was thirsty, I spent the whole time kicking up a fuss because I wanted a lemonade but didn't want to miss a minute of the game. My dad always had a lot of trust in me, so he decided – Daddy gets the lemonade, daughter stays on her own on the terrace, but doesn't budge from the spot.

I spent the first five minutes on my own, standing still like a good girl. But then I shifted a bit to my left – I wanted to get closer to the corner flag. Even then, I was a huge fan of corner kicks, I just love it, the way a well-struck corner curls in the air. And then a bit further left. And a bit further. And then I went up a few steps. But suddenly, there was the fence and a fat man, blocking my view at the exact moment the Eintracht player kicked his corner. I went up a few more steps. I had a great view, the corner became a goal, huge cheers, the celebrations carried me along with them somewhere, and I stayed there.

At half-time, I remembered my dad. I wanted to go back to our spot but couldn't find it. I had no idea where we'd been standing, everything looked so much the same. I fought my way through the crowd, right and left again, up and down again, but I couldn't find my dad and I didn't see any more of the match either, no corners, no goals, no celebrations. I knew my dad would be roaming the stand too, looking for me, and that it was all because I hadn't done as he'd said. In the end, I ran to the ticket office and they called my dad.

He was there at once. He didn't scold, just took me in his arms, and: wept. Later, he always claimed he'd been crying because Eintracht had conceded a goal in the ninetieth minute and lost the match.

And now something falls on my neck from behind.

'Darling! Look who I've brought!'

Carla.

Oh my God. Carla.

She looks rough, tousled hair, rumpled face, she's still wearing the same thin dress as the day before yesterday, she smells of pub, but she's beaming. I can hardly take in the fact that she's here, I don't believe it, I just look at her, and very slowly I realise that she's fine and still has all her arms and legs.

'Oh man,' I say. 'Oh man. Where were you?'

'I've been out with Scott and James,' she says.

'Who are Scott and James?'

She tilts her head and pulls two guys over, one on her left, one on her right, and says 'These guys. This is Scott and James.'

Scott and James are built like tanks. They're tall, broad-shouldered, dark-haired, wearing thin sweatshirts and Celtic scarves, and they look absolutely identical. Scott might have a few more freckles than James, and is maybe a dash more handsome, if handsome is quite the word for absolute units like these. But they look fun, you have to give them that.

'*Hey ya*,' they say, almost simultaneously.

'*Hey, you*,' I say, somewhat confused.

'Scott's my new boyfriend,' says Carla, kissing him, he almost crushes her. Aha.

'I couldn't sleep on Thursday night,' she says, 'and in the end, I got back up and went out again, and I met these two in the Schanze, they came in on a ship, from Glasgow, you know, Scotland.'

'Uh-huh,' I say. Is she thinking that just because I might have Scottish ancestry somewhere in my American family tree, that'll help me fall for these hulks right away?

'OK...?' I say.

'We had an amazing night and a great day,' she says, 'and

then I stayed over with the boys in their hotel and, well, you know how it goes, sweetie.'

I don't, but I don't care so long as she's happy and alive, and she certainly seems to be.

'Beer?' she asks.

Scott and James nod, I decline, I think I've had enough in the last few days. I'd rather have a cup of tea, but I don't want to admit that in public just now. Carla goes for beer, the match is about to begin and I'm slowly starting to feel better, all in all.

'Yeah,' says James, and Scott says, 'Yeah.'

The whole business strikes me as deeply weird, but in the end Sankt Pauli lose again and I'd say that my world is OK, albeit a slightly more stressful version of itself than normal.

At home, I don't even manage to switch the light on. I kick my boots into a corner, let my coat, my jeans and my jumper drop onto the floor, and fall into bed, into a deep, dark sleep.

I do hear the knock on my door, but it's so far away, and because I know that Klatsche will get by fine without me, I go under.

You should go to sleep
I told her
but she didn't want to
she didn't shut her eyes
she scratched me and
she was unkind
she didn't understand
that it won't work if
she won't sleep
I didn't want to hurt her but
she kept on scratching and
how am I meant to do it if
she's scratching the whole time and
so then I
held her and
put the necklace on her
and so then
she did sleep
like an angel
with the pink hair and then
I laid her on the beach
like an angel
and so then
she could rest
like an angel

because
it'd been exhausting and
then she liked it there
on the beach

MY FATHER'S HEART

I'm standing in a tiny, dark room. My father is standing beside me, he's much taller than me and he's holding my hand. We're alone. A dull thudding drones through my body. Right in front of us, a door opens in the wall, behind the door there's a narrow corridor with a strangely warm yet pallid light falling through it. My father's hand grows uneasy, it starts to tremble and blurs, it softens and loses its contours, it's getting hard to keep hold of it. I try all the same and somehow it works, but it costs energy. At the end of the corridor, the silhouette of a woman appears, in a flowing dress. The woman has no face but I know: she's looking at us. And I know who she is. My father's hand dissolves in my hand, the female figure turns and walks away from us, she distances herself from us ever further, she leaves us, she doesn't even look around, and eventually she's vanished. The door shuts again but there's still a little light creeping around the crack, an inkling. Something falls to the floor. It's lying at my feet, it's about the size of a fist, it's warm and wet and glinting, it's my father's heart.

MORE WEEPING WILLOWS BACK THERE

It's not a nice way to wake up. My pulse is pecking at the inside of my throat in exasperation. Outside, it's still dark but the birds are already awake. That helps a little. I stand up, walk to the bathroom and shower the night off my skin. Then I get dressed and head out onto the street.

The Kiez is empty, like someone swept all the people away. There's only the rubbish lying around the place like the remains of a cheap firework. That's often the way early on a Sunday morning. The party people don't seem to hold out as long on Saturdays as on Fridays, most of them are still feeling Thursday in their bones. And those who do hold out have popped pills and are hidden behind the steel doors of the after-party.

I turn up my coat collar, but that's really just a gesture. It's not at all cold, the air feels surprisingly warm. The sky is slowly breaking up, fine, bright cracks are appearing, I send up a greeting. Hey, Dad. How are you?

Obviously, I'm not expecting an answer, I'm not crazy. But I could do with talking to him, yeah, I'd like that a lot. Shit, I can't even visit him at the cemetery. He's walled up in

Belhaven, North Carolina. After his death, I had the feeling
that it would be sensible to take him back to where he came
from, so I splashed out on a trip home for him. And now he's
there and I'm here, and I haven't been sure that that was right
for a long time now. Because I'm never going back to
Belhaven ever again. Belhaven is a shithole.

*

Back then, I flew into Washington D.C. and then took the
train south, with an urn and a bottle of vodka in my
luggage. I really did drink a lot in those weeks. My father's
four cousins, so some kind of aunts of mine, wore bright
dresses and blow-dried hairstyles, their husbands were
morose and red-faced, and drank bourbon incessantly.
Their children were silly teenagers with croaky voices, and
the whole lot of them made me want to puke. I couldn't
see even a trace of my father in any of these people. But at
least there was never-ending bourbon.

The funeral took place at the local cemetery, beneath
weeping willows; it was humid, the cousins wore hideous
hats on top of their blow-dries, a fat man, some kind of tenor,
sang the American national anthem. The mourners were
mostly men from the US army who claimed to be 'old
friends', I'd never heard of any of them. In spirit, I was con-
tinually apologising to my dad because he would have hated
all this. I'd wanted to do the right thing but everything about
it was wrong. I'd brought him back to a country where he

hadn't been at home for a long time, and I'd had him shoved into a wall. He'd have been much better off on my window-sill.

After the funeral, there was greasy food at the house of Cousin Grace and her husband, Luke. I tried to chat to people, but that didn't work out for long, so I slipped one of Luke's bourbon bottles under my coat and said goodbye to my relations. Grace called me a taxi. Her hug took my breath away and, for the first time that day, I started to cry.

'Oh, honey,' said Grace, stroking my hair, 'oh, honey, take care, honey.'

But then she didn't know what else to say, we didn't know each other, after all. I think they were all glad when the tragi-comic character from Europe finally disappeared again.

I let the taxi driver take me to the only hotel in Belhaven. I'd booked a room from Germany because there was no way I wanted to stay with my relatives. But all I could think, when I got out of the taxi with my bag in one hand and Luke's bottle in the other, was: wow, shit.

The River Forest Manor looked like the Bates Motel in Southern fancy dress. Dark and terrifying. I walked up the massive front steps, paid the concierge sixty dollars in advance, stepped into a stinking lift and sank, in my room, into a dark-red carpet. I put down my bag, drew the greasy, brown velvet curtains aside, opened the dismal window, sat down on the windowsill, breathed in the humid air, ah, more weeping willows back there.

I set the bottle to my lips and only set it down again when

I really couldn't manage any more, then I lay down on top of the burgundy bedspread without getting undressed, and dozed through the night.

In the morning, the taste in my mouth was as though I'd bitten into a grave, but even so, for a moment I considered visiting my mother in Wisconsin, after all, I was closer to her than I'd been in eighteen years, since she'd run off with that moron of a major and abandoned my father and me. I imagined what it would be like to ring her doorbell, to look the way I looked now, and to say: hello, I buried my father yesterday, the guy you had a daughter with, do you remember? He never got over you leaving us. He died of a broken heart. And the way I feel, I wish I'd died with him. What do you say to that?

I didn't travel to Wisconsin. I took the next flight back to Frankfurt, sold our flat, rented a little attic and started a law degree; over the next few years, I cultivated my ever-stabilising fear of commitment. Even before my father died, I hadn't exactly been a woman for light-hearted love affairs. But after his death, I spent what must have been five years keeping away from anything that could put me in danger. And the things I did try, now and then, aren't really worth mentioning. I'd call myself more of the inaccessible type – don't mess with that shit and it won't hurt you.

I keep wondering what would have become of me if I'd stayed in Belhaven after the funeral, if I'd tried, out of sheer sentimentality, to make a life there. I didn't want that, not for a single moment, but the state I was in back then, my goodness, anything would have been possible, maybe even getting stuck in North Carolina. Before I visited Belhaven for the first, and hopefully last, time, I had always thought of the place as some kind of homeland. I'd long had the feeling that I might be able to find something there that was missing from my life. A home.

So, yeah.

In the end, I did at least bring back a heap of useful information from Belhaven: 1) If you've never had a home, you'll never find one. 2) Your relatives aren't always the best family you can get. 3) The River Forest Manor is the world's worst hotel.

*

I walk and walk and walk, and meanwhile I've ended up on the beach at the Elbstrand, the river is choppy, crashing on the shore. There's quite a wind blowing, the grass on the bank is lying almost flat over the stones, and the sand is blowing up in little eddies. In summer, people lie here sunbathing and play frisbee and barbecue things, it's pandemonium, but a nice kind of pandemonium. Hard to imagine, seeing the beach as lonely, as gloomy, as it looks now. It really ought to have been day for some time at this point, but the wind's now whipping dark clouds across the sky, letting no light through. There'll either be a storm today or a constant state of twilight. But it's OK walking through the sand like this and watching the Elbe, it comforts me, as ever. Over there, where it heads towards the ocean, a container ship is on its way to the North Sea.

Sometimes, when you think things are about to get better, they suddenly get much worse. I walk faster so as to be able to see better. There's something lying in the sand, maybe thirty metres from me.

He's put a pink wig on her, long, smooth, glossy plastic hair, which is spilling into the sand. She's tall and athletic, her legs are stretched straight as an arrow, her arms are spread out. Her eyes are closed, her face is looking up to heaven. Running around her neck is the same sharp strangulation mark that ran around Margarete's and Henriette's necks too.

I sit beside the dead woman, pull out my telephone and call my police colleagues. It starts raining, fast and hard and merciless. I take off my coat, lay it over the body, stay sitting beside her and wait for the others to get here at last.

HELL

Faller's the first to get to me.

'My God, Chastity,' he says, 'what are you doing here at this time?'

I can't speak. I can only look at him. The water's running down my face, I don't know if it comes from the rain or if it could be tears. I suppose it could, but I'd be surprised. My tears haven't made it back to the surface since my father's funeral.

Faller pulls me up and holds me tight, discreetly.

'You're shaking,' he says.

Brückner and Calabretta come stamping over, bringing SOCO and Mr Borger with them. Brückner's wearing a baseball cap, Calabretta's got a Corleone hat on, Mr Borger has a raincoat. SOCO are wearing the usual white overalls, Hollerieth has an umbrella which he doesn't put up. No point, not in this wind.

'Here's a thing,' says Hollerieth, pushing me away from the corpse. Faller rumbles and stays very close beside me.

'What the hell are you doing here, Chas?' he asks me again, offering me a Roth-Händle.

'I couldn't sleep,' I say, well what d'you know, I can speak again, 'so I went for a bit of a walk.'

Brückner and Calabretta are with us now.

'Did you find her, boss?' asks Calabretta. He's still got a bit of his croissant between his teeth. I light the cigarette that Faller gave me, and nod.

'Not a nice thing,' says Brückner, pushing back his cap.

'What's with the coat?' hisses Hollerieth, holding my trench coat under my nose.

'I don't know myself,' I say, 'it started raining so suddenly and I felt sorry for her.'

Hollerieth shakes his head. 'I'm sorry too.'

'You can take the coat back to the lab with you if you like,' I say.

And so we stand smoking in the rain. It's nearly seven. I feel like a cardboard cut-out and can't think. From the corner of my eye, I watch what the men from SOCO are doing to the dead woman. Right now, some of them are masking her off from top to bottom with wide sticky tape, while others are combing the surrounding area, putting up barriers and taking photos.

'Shit,' says Brückner, 'looks like the press is on its way.'

Seems like Patschinski had a bad night's sleep too and spent the whole morning listening to the police radio. Wouldn't be good for him to see me like this.

'Calabretta,' says Faller, 'take the boss here away. Brückner, you stay on the scene. I'll look after our friend from the paper.'

'Thanks,' I say to Faller, and nod to Calabretta.

'That's OK,' he says.

I glance back at the dead woman. Lying there like that, she looks like an angel. And everyone here knows that tomorrow, all hell will break loose.

I DO THE FISH HERE

Calabretta holds the passenger door of his patrol car for me, I get in, he shuts the door from the outside. It's as though everything is only happening to me, as though I can no longer do anything for myself.

Once Calabretta's got in and started the engine, he says: 'I've never found a body.'

'Don't worry,' I say, 'that will come.'

He stares through the windscreen.

'I could use a coffee,' he says. 'How about you?'

'Excellent idea,' I say. 'Where?'

'Let me surprise you,' he says, revving up and driving in the direction of the fish market. My general impression is that he loves the fish market and is on the best of terms with most of the traders.

'Calabretta,' I say.

'Yes?'

'No eel and no houseplants, OK?'

'No fish slurry, no rubber trees, no tourist tat. I promise. Just somewhere good. Deal?'

'Deal,' I say.

As we drive, the rain eases up a bit. And it gradually dawns on me what just happened. We've got a third dead woman, and I practically fell over her. If only I'd stayed in bed.

'*Ecco*,' says Calabretta, turning into a yard just below the Altonaer Balkon, where he parks up. 'We're here.'

We're by a warehouse delivery ramp and a closed set of steel double doors.

'We're here?' I ask.

'Let's go,' he says, jumping out of the car, 'come on.'

I get out and smooth down my clammy clothes. Calabretta climbs onto the ramp and hammers three times on the metal door. It opens immediately. A little guy in a white coat grins at us. He has dark, thinning hair, a hooked nose and sparkling green eyes.

'Vito!' he cries.

'Totó!' cries Calabretta, no less joyfully. As if one of the two of them had just come home from the frontline. He beckons me over, holds out his hand and pulls me onto the ramp.

'Boss,' he says, 'allow me to introduce you to my friend Salvatore.'

I shake hands with Salvatore and allow his smile and his small, wonky teeth to bowl me over.

'Totó,' Calabretta says to his friend Salvatore, 'allow me to introduce you to my boss.'

'Ah, boss,' says Salvatore, and I get the feeling that he's about— Yes: he spreads out his arms and hugs me.

'I've heard a lot about you, boss. I do the fish here. *Caffè*?'

Calabretta and I nod synchronously, and for the first time in days, it feels like it's me inside my skin again. Salvatore vanishes back through the doors, Calabretta rubs his hands warm and sticks them in the pockets of his leather jacket, which is, as ever, far too tight.

'Thanks,' I say.

'What for?'

'You know,' I say, 'for this. This is good.'

'Ah,' he says, 'I just can't stand it when a friend is sad.'

I stare at the tips of my toes.

'I know,' he says, 'there are some pains that you can never quite get off your chest, but a good coffee eases all that a little, believe me.'

'Won't make it any worse, at any rate,' I say, elbowing him in the side.

The door swings open and Salvatore reappears with a tray. On the tray are three thick, white espresso cups, and in the cups is something dark and viscous.

'*Salute*,' says Calabretta.

'*Salute*,' says Totó.

'*Cheers*,' I say, and we drink.

Perhaps the leather-jacketed commissario and I just formed a flimsy bond.

OK, LET'S DRIVE TO THE SEASIDE

It's stopped raining. Outside the house I bump into
Klatsche. He's got a bag of bread rolls under his arm. He
squeezes my shoulder and gives me a kiss on the cheek.

'Did you get wet?'

I nod.

'Been out for an early-morning walk or what?'

I nod.

'Can you still speak?'

I nod.

'Then say something.'

'Good morning,' I say.

'Don't believe you,' he says.

'Where are you going with those rolls?' I ask.

'To yours,' he says. 'People can eat breakfast together at the
weekend now and again when they're friends, you know?'

'It rings a bell,' I say.

'OK,' he says. 'Then let's go back to mine, eat a few Sunday
rolls and have a bit of a chat.'

'OK,' I say.

Klatsche's place is more of a tool museum than a flat. There are all kinds of metal things on the walls in every room. I have no idea what they're all called. He always says he can't help it, he just has a heart of steel, and he maintains that without his tools he feels incomplete. I can kind of understand that.

His wobbly kitchen table is made of old junk welded together, you have to take constant care that your coffee cup doesn't tip over. The chairs are from the same collection, the difference being that you have to take care that you don't tip over yourself.

When I tell him what's happened, he puts down his cheese roll. His coffee cup wobbles.

'Let's drive to the seaside,' he says.

'Don't be silly,' I say. 'I've got very different shit in my head.'

'Exactly,' he says. 'And that's not good. Today's Sunday. Come on, let's go.'

'Can I just pop over and brush my teeth?'

'Seeing as it's you,' he says.

When I stand up, my cup tips over and everything spills across the table.

THEY CAN'T SAY MORE PRECISELY

Seven minutes later, we're sitting in the Volvo. Two hours and three traffic jams later, we're at the Baltic. Five hours and a walk on the beach later, we're standing by a fishing boat, eating herring rolls. Six hours and a chewing gum later, we're kissing in the dunes. Seven hours later, we're still lying there. Nine hours later, we get out of the Volvo, back in Sankt Pauli again, and hold hands. Nine hours and fifteen minutes later, we're sitting in a pub. It's half past seven on a Sunday evening.

The woman behind the bar has plaited her red hair into loop braids. We order hot chocolate. The bar is in old, dark wood – generations of people have sat here and held fast to it. Hanging from the ceiling are plush lampshades. Dim light. It's a little overheated and smells of cigarettes. Through the fogged-up window, we can see that it's getting cold outside.

But then my phone rings. I slip off the barstool and walk outside the door. Brückner. He sounds tired.

'How's it looking?' I ask.

'Our man's getting careless,' he says.

'Meaning?'

'He drove over the sand in his car. We've got tyre prints. They're from a four-by-four, a large, heavy thing, European design, BMW or Mercedes or Porsche Cayenne.'

'They can't say more precisely?' I ask.

'No,' he says. 'But there are now a couple of poor blokes hunting down the owners of every shitty four-wheel drive in this city.'

'OK,' I say, 'what else?'

'Forensics say there was a struggle this time. The victim had a lot of bruises, especially on her forearms. He probably had to sit on them to be able to strangle her with the cable tie. And the DNA from the skin particles under her nails matches that of the hair we found on Henriette Auer's body.'

'Any DNA match in the database?'

'No such luck,' he says, 'we haven't met this guy before.'

'Why did he get into a fight?' I ask. 'I thought he was shy.'

'Could be that the barbiturate didn't work properly this time,' he says. 'Betty Kirschtein says that if the victim was a pill popper or an epileptic that's quite possible. But to find out, they need to do a few more tests.'

'And what does Mr Borger say to that?' I ask.

'He says another possibility is that the killer got impatient and couldn't wait for her to pass out. Either way, this time it was a nasty affair.'

'Whew,' I say, 'sounds bad.'

'Yes,' says Brückner, crumpled.

'When do the doctors say she died?'

'Same as the other two women, between midnight and four in the morning.'

'Do we know who she was yet?' I ask.

'I went straight to the Acapulco,' he says. 'She was a dancer there.'

'He really is getting careless,' I say. 'What was the woman's name, and how old was she?'

'Sandrine Janssen,' he says. 'She was twenty-seven, had been dancing in the Kiez for almost six years. Was kind of the *grande dame* at the Acapulco. The girls there have really lost it now, and so's their boss. They're considering shutting up shop.'

'We have to get them to carry on a few days more,' I say, 'from now on, we shadow the Acapulco round the clock. And in the evenings, when it's in operation, we'll need the specialists. Will you send two men along?'

'Already on it,' he says. 'They must be getting into position about now.'

PLAIN CLOTHES

When I wake up, Klatsche's already gone, but his shirt is hanging over my chair. On my desk, there's a note:

Out and about.

See you this evening?

I make coffee, have a shower and then make my way through the rain to the police HQ.

'Lousy weather,' says the taxi driver.

I don't answer, just look out of the window as we drive through the Schanzenviertel.

An old gentleman is coming towards us on a shining, silver folding bicycle, he's wearing a perfectly fitting cream suit, his grey hair is accurately parted, he's sitting on his bike like it's a show horse, and as if the sun were above us and not the eternal grey. Then a man of about the same age on a rusty, ochre folding bike. His clothes look like they've been freshly plucked from a rag bag, he's wearing several layers of knackered garments yet still looks very thin. On his head is a dark-blue knitted cap, while gummed-up strands of brown hair peep out at the sides. His glasses have thick lenses that are so smeary it must be impossible for him to make out the road. Now here comes a young man on a black Dutch bicycle. There's a small platform over the front wheel. Lying on the platform is a violin case, beside which sits a small boy in a red raincoat. Coming along behind him is a woman of about sixty in an electric wheelchair. She's wearing double denim and huge, dark sunglasses, and her bleached blonde hair is piled into a towering up-do; there's an HSV flag fastened to the backrest of her chair, the flag is huge and square, easily one metre fifty each way, and it's fluttering in the wind.

The table in our team office looks like a newsagent's counter – I don't even have to look at the headlines to know that they're all asking the same questions: how many more women have to die? When will this lunatic get put away? How useless are our police?

Calabretta's reading the local rag and I can see that it's getting to him. Betty Kirschtein isn't there. I guess she's doing the drug tests that Brückner mentioned yesterday.

'*Moin*, guys,' I say.

'*Moin*, boss,' say the guys.

'Read the paper?' asks Faller.

'No,' I say. 'How bad is it?'

'Very,' says Schulle. 'We're officially morons.'

'Then let's get a move on,' I say, 'and show them all that we're not morons. What do we know about the third murder?'

'The most important thing is the tyre prints,' says Brückner. 'And that we definitely have the killer's skin under the victim's fingernails.'

'Has the undercover team from yesterday reported back yet?' I ask.

'Yes,' says Faller. 'Nobody caught their eye. But one team will now spend its entire evenings in the Acapulco. We've spoken to the owner, and he's promised to keep the place running, despite the murders. The girls are brave and ready to act as bait. They know we'll be there, and they'll go with anyone who chats them up. If he's to fall into our trap, the Acapulco will have to play along, and they understand that. They want the bloke caught.'

'What else?' I ask.

'We're not just watching the Acapulco, but all the other relevant dance clubs, just to be on the safe side,' says Schulle. 'And as of an hour ago, there are several plain-clothes units out there, checking the tyres of every matching four-by-four in Hamburg, and speaking to the owners.'

'Am I glad that I'm not part of a plain-clothes unit,' I say.

Then I head to the prosecution service, to think.

TIDY

My office looks like a bomb went off in it. I don't have a
cleaner because I don't want anyone but me to come near
my files, but that means I have to look after my few square
metres of floorspace myself. As I haven't done so for at
least two months, the dust is now lying in layers, the pa-
perwork is piling up in every corner, and I've trodden any
amount of Hamburg weather into my office too. OK, so
I'll get cracking, and while I do, I'll have a think.

Start with the files, they need shelving.

And then there's this man who scalps women. That clearly
scares me. Scares me so much that I haven't been able to get
to grips with him yet. I'm just running around like a CID
hanger-on and I'm not getting anywhere with the part that's
actually my job, the thing I'm really good at – being the idea
behind the investigation. I know my colleagues are patient
and used to waiting for my head to catch up, but I'm starting
to lose patience myself.

So, the files are on the shelf.

Now the old newspapers, they go in the bin.

Three women are dead now, and that Basso – this has to

stop, I need an idea, a feeling for the killer, because I know this: once I've managed to create a sense of him in my head, we'll get him. That's irrational, but it works. It's always worked so far. I just have to push away my fear and fire up my imagination, really see into his world for a brief moment, really look at him. No idea where I got this skill. One day, I just noticed that I could. I think it's a child's skill – grasping stories with your soul. And for some reason, I kept the ability. Maybe because there wasn't anything else in my childhood worth salvaging.

I get an old duster out of the cupboard where I keep my personal shit and dust down my desk, then move on to the windowsills and shelves.

So he sees her. He looks at her. He picks her out. Something about her attracts him. The thing that links all three victims is their beauty, their beautiful hair. Dancers use it to emphasise their movements, to amplify the beauty. So he looks at a woman who has that – has beautiful hair. The yearning for it must be enormous, almost painful, there must be a big gap within him, a hole. There must have been something there once, something capable of tearing such a hole, otherwise he wouldn't miss it so badly.

I put the duster away in the cupboard again and pull out the mini handheld vacuum cleaner that I stored here some time ago. I get down on my knees and start, bit by bit, to vacuum the floor. This is going to take a while.

Mr Borger said he's not doing this for the sake of killing, or he'd do it differently, more brutally. Someone who wants to kill spills blood. The blood means nothing to him. He just wants their hair.

He speaks to her. Friendly, caring, admiring. She likes that and they get chatting. She even goes with him. It doesn't matter exactly what he says to her. The way he says it, that must be it, the admiration in his words, which is probably completely genuine. He must be a non-scary kind of guy or she wouldn't go with him. Maybe he seems a little lonely, like someone you'd want to help, and more or less like the kind of person you could easily put in his place if he did get too pushy. And he must be very different from the men these girls usually have to deal with in their rough world. There's something attractive about someone who seems pleasant.

He takes her to where he's alone with her, he takes her back to his home. He might live quite close by, right here in the Kiez, she knows the ground, feels safe there. He offers her refreshment, an after-work drink, and she accepts gladly, that'll hit the spot. He stirs the tablets into the drink and watches as she slowly drifts off. Once she stops moving, no longer reacts to his voice, he puts the cable tie around her neck and pulls it tight. He doesn't like to do that, doesn't enjoy it, but he has to be certain he isn't hurting her. And it's quick with a cable tie, you don't have to grip it for long, you just pull it tight for a moment. Maybe she twitches, maybe her body rears up again, he doesn't watch. When it's over, he undresses her, he wants to see her skin, smell her, have her very close to him, maybe he lays his head on her chest for a moment. Then he gets the knife and, very carefully, does what he has to do, bit by bit he takes her hair, and because it has to stay intact, he has to take her skin too. It churns him up, he knows it's wrong, but he can't help it. Once he's got the hair, he puts the wig on her. As if nothing has ever happened. He hasn't done any harm, it all looks fine. And then he takes her away, to a place that suits her, where she's sure to be happy. It's as though he's burying her, bidding her farewell.

He puts her hair carefully aside. It's his treasure, for a moment it fills the hideous holes in his life, and for a few days he feels a little better. The pressure is off for a while.

I close my eyes. My heart is pounding. It's happening: I can imagine him. I know how he feels. It's terrible. He's suffering like a dog and doesn't even know what's wrong with him. I could cry.

When I open my eyes again, I'm sitting on the floor by my desk, and I have to say: my office is A+ tidy now.

WHY DO WE KEEP MEETING LIKE THIS

Carla's café is rammed full of people, Scott's standing behind the counter, cutting croissants and filling them with cheese and ham, and the sad Portuguese music that Carla loves so much is softening up people's heads. Scott throws me a smile, Carla emerges from the kitchen, takes my hand and pulls me into the corner by the loo.

'Isn't he great?'

She's beaming.

'He's working here like he's never done anything else, he says he wants to stay in Hamburg, and the sex is awesome, I'm telling you...'

'Carla,' I say.

'Why didn't you tell me that two more girls have been murdered?'

'You weren't here,' I say, 'you were off on a bender.'

She shrugs her shoulders.

'How about you? What's happening with Zandvoort?'

'Nothing,' I say. 'I slept with Klatsche on Thursday night.'

'Oh,' she says. 'That's great, you're a great couple.'

'We're a funny couple,' I say. 'If we're one at all.'

'You might want to have a quick think about that,' she says, 'look who's coming in.'

I turn around. Zandvoort is standing in the door. He's wearing a pale-grey sharkskin suit and a black scarf, and has a minimalist smile. He looks good.

'True,' I say, 'I ought to make it clear to him that he's not getting anything from me.'

'And I ought to bring you a coffee,' she says.

Zandvoort sits at a table by the window. I walk over to him and say: 'Hello.'

Carla brings me my coffee.

'One for me too, please,' says Zandvoort.

His voice sounds husky. He leans back.

'What's up?' I ask, sitting down.

He pulls a black cigarette case from his jacket pocket and lays it on the table.

'Why do we keep meeting like this?' he asks. 'I didn't expect you to be here.'

I drink a sip of my coffee and say: 'I'm always here. Why *do* we keep meeting like this?'

'No idea,' he says.

Carla brings him a cup of coffee.

'You see,' I say, 'neither have I.'

'Come and have dinner with me,' he says, 'around seven. There's no performance on at the Okzidental this evening, so I'm free.'

Heaven knows what gets into me, but I say, 'All right.' Perhaps I just want to see how he reacts if you take him by surprise.

He responds coolly and drinks his coffee quite at his leisure.

Later, on the way to work, I call my secretary and ask her to see what she can dig up about Zandvoort. If I can't manage to keep him at a distance, I want at least to know exactly who I'm dealing with. And by the time I reach my insanely clean office, there are a few photocopied newspaper articles waiting for me on my extremely tidy desk. Zandvoort was once a high-profile young director. He tended to work in smaller venues, not the major theatres, but it was all very promising, he was considered a big talent. Then there was a turning point, about twenty years ago, when interest in him dropped off, his productions got boring apparently, a female critic called them 'self-righteous'. Then, seven years ago, he took on an artistic directorship in Aachen, his home city. And he's been running the Okzidental for six months. He told an interviewer that it was 'a seriously exciting project', but of course that's nonsense. I wonder what he's doing here and why he didn't just stay in Aachen.

PROPERTY SHIT LIGHTING

Just before seven, I'm standing outside Zandvoort's place. A new apartment block in steel and glass, impressive, prestigious port-view location. This kind of thing costs megabucks. How much does the director of a Kiez theatre earn? I've been standing here for five minutes now, unable to make up my mind whether to ring the bell or walk away again. But something in my head says: ring. So I ring the bell marked *C. Zandvoort*, and the door immediately snaps open. Was he watching me just now? And if so, from where?

I take the lift to the fifth floor.

Zandvoort is standing in his doorway, wearing a black jumper and black trousers. Next to the door, a spiral staircase leads up to another flat. Down by the front door, Zandvoort's was the topmost name tag.

'I was afraid you'd never ring.'

I look at him in confusion, he invites me in, I clock the intercom beside the door and understand – right next to the handset, there's a little screen that shows the street.

'You looked like you were afraid of being followed,' he says.

'Should I be?' I ask, taking off my trench coat and pressing it into Zandvoort's hand.

'Not that I know of,' he says, hanging my coat on the coat rack. The hallway isn't large, but it's cool and unwelcoming, there's nothing here but the coat rack and us.

Standing in the living room is a large steel table, standing on the table is a five-branch candlestick in chrome. The candles are illuminating a least 150 euros' worth of sushi. I like raw fish, but I dislike it when someone starts off by dishing up this kind of thing. Pizza would have been fine.

'Fancy,' I say.

He walks to the table and picks up two filled glasses.

'I hope you like champagne.'

To be honest, no.

He presses a glass into my hand.

I feel a sudden need to be as rude as possible. 'Thanks,' I say and start drinking before he can raise his glass in reply. Zandvoort looks suitably piqued. Maybe he's on the point of kicking me back out again and, hey, that would suit me perfectly. I walk to the window, a wide, floor-to-ceiling glass frontage. Port, docks, ships, containers. Not bad.

'Nice view,' I say.

'I know,' he says, and I can sense him studying my shoulders. I feel insecure with the dark, smooth granite floor beneath my feet, I'm surrounded by anthracite walls and hanging over me are grey ceilings with inset spotlights. Something makes me shiver.

'Are you cold?'

Suddenly, he's standing very close behind me.

I take a small step to the side.

'Got a cigarette?' I ask.

'Of course,' he says, walks to the dining table and opens a drawer.

'What would you like?' he asks, 'Dunhill, Marlboro?'

'Lucky Strike?' I ask.

'You're in luck,' he says holding up a packet of Luckies. What's he got in that drawer? A fag machine? He gives me a cigarette and a light.

'Thanks,' I say, drawing the smoke deep into my lungs.

'Do you have children?' he asks.

'No.'

'Siblings?'

'No.'

'An ex-husband?'

'No.'

'Do you like your job?'

'Most of the time.'

'What do you like doing when nobody's looking?'

'Falling over,' I say.

'Are you sick?'

'What is this?' I ask. 'A quiz?'

'I'm just trying,' he says, 'to get to know you a little.'

'Forget it,' I say.

'Let's eat.'

It sounds like an order.

I walk to the table and sit on a chair at the far end. Once

again, I've found myself feeling like prey in his company. Why did I come here?

He sits at the other end of the table. There's a good three metres between us.

'Please, help yourself,' he says.

I take a little salmon and two spicy tuna rolls from the platter right in front of me. He reaches for the cuttlefish and caviar.

'Oh,' he says, 'excuse me.' He stands up, walks into the kitchen and comes back with two glasses and a bottle of Chardonnay.

'White, if I remember rightly?'

It's as though Zandvoort has appended a smile to his face. I wonder what he was doing in the kitchen.

'Yes, thanks,' I say, and when he's sitting down again, I have another go at courtesy, it must be possible just to sit here and eat dinner together, millions of people do that every day.

'How's the theatre going?' I ask.

'What exactly do you want to know?'

'Is it sold out?' I ask. 'Are you managing to get the place all spruced up again?'

'The performances are full,' he says, popping a piece of squid and rice into his mouth. 'Do you go to the theatre?'

'No,' I say. 'Theatre isn't really my thing.'

'What is your thing then?'

'Football,' I say, 'but you know that.'

I'm relaxing a little.

'And what else are you interested in?' he asks.

'Criminals,' I say. Then I end this second Q&A with a double slice of salmon. Zandvoort watches as I chew and my tension immediately rises again, his predatoriness is seriously getting on my nerves, and it's only the last remnants of good manners within me that stop me from just spitting the salmon back out again. But I'm now seriously looking for an elegant opportunity to get out of here fast.

It's all so awkward.

Zandvoort looks at the door and suddenly *he* seems to be finding something awkward.

'Hello, son,' he says. His voice sounds icy.

I didn't hear anyone come in. I turn around. Standing in the living-room doorway is a man of maybe twenty-eight, in a thin, dark-blue jumper and faded jeans. He has short brown hair, a pale, slender face and a dashing birthmark right over his top lip. This is the boy from the jetties. He's acting like a foal in the panther enclosure.

'John,' says Zandvoort, 'I have a guest.'

The boy says nothing, he just looks at me.

'Hello,' I say.

I try a smile, but it doesn't work. His effect on me isn't quite as dramatic as on Friday, when I saw him huddled on the bollard, but something within me screams at the sight of him. He does a clumsy about-turn and vanishes as quickly as he appeared. Did he recognise me or not?

'Sorry about that,' says Zandvoort, 'my son's not exactly the life and soul.'

'He seems a bit perturbed,' I say.

'Mm,' says Zandvoort, turning back to his sushi. It's like the boy was never here.

'Where's his mother?' I ask.

'Dead,' he says.

'Oh,' I say.

'Car crash, a good ten years ago. We'd met a year before that and just married.'

I must look a little confused, I could have sworn that the boy I just saw was a lot older than eleven.

'He's not my son by birth,' he says. 'I adopted him after his mother died. There was no family and otherwise he'd have had to go into a home.'

'That was very generous of you,' I say, 'taking him in. Not everyone would have done that.'

'You try telling him that,' he says. 'He doesn't thank me for it.'

Whoa there.

'Does he live here with you?' I ask.

'He has the attic,' he says, 'and he works as a lighting technician at my theatre. Well. His lighting is properly shit, to be honest.'

OK. I've had it. I put my chopsticks aside and stand up.

'You know what,' I say, 'I ought to get going.'

He leans back, sips his wine and says: 'Oh, really?'

'Yes,' I say.

'You disappoint me,' he says, 'I thought you had more to offer.'

'Ah well,' I say, 'you were out of luck.'

I walk to the coat rack and take my coat. Just before I close the door behind me, I catch Zandvoort saying: 'See you, Chastity.'

I walk down the stairs and once I'm outside, I see, over the road, a four-by-four that wasn't there before. It's a Porsche Cayenne.

I write down the registration because you never know.

LEITMOTIV

I sit on a bench on my street and smoke a cigarette. There's a light on still at Klatsche's.

NUMBER PLATE

The light blinks through the curtains. Klatsche's face is full of fondness and ease, and his hair is sticking up in all directions.

'I have to go,' I say, 'there's something I have to—'

'*Bullshit*,' he says, standing up and pulling the curtains to let the day into the room. He walks into the kitchen and makes coffee, I can hear him tinkering with the espresso pot as I watch the gulls outside the window. Some things are just very hard to defend yourself against.

On the way to the police station, I call Schulle.

'Boss,' he says.

'Where are you? HQ?'

'Yep.'

'Could you do me a favour?' I ask.

'Sure,' he says.

'I need someone to check a number plate.'

'No problem,' says Schulle.

I give him the number of the four-by-four that I saw outside Zandvoort's building yesterday evening. He promises to call me right back. Ten minutes later, my phone rings.

'I've got the owner,' he says.

'And?'

'The car was licensed six months ago in Aachen. It belongs to a Claudius Zandvoort.'

'Wow,' I say.

'What?' asks Schulle.

'Nothing,' I say, 'thanks.'

RUSTLE SOMETHING UP

Faller is sitting in his office, digging in various dusty files that look about fifty years old. When he sees me in the doorway, he claps them shut.

'What are you looking for?' I ask.

'Tell you later,' he says, reaching for the telephone and calling the surveillance boys. He tells them I'm here and asks them to pop over for a moment.

'How are you, Chas?' he asks.

'Well, that,' I say, 'is for me to tell *you* later.'

He smiles and lights a Roth-Händle.

Then the door opens. The shadows are here. These guys are like magic, their chief seems to deploy his men by look. According to whether they're needed in Blankenese or Sankt Pauli. The two he's parked at the Acapulco are perfect for the job. One is about fifty and looks like an over-the-hill businessman. He's wearing a tatty, navy-blue suit that's too short in the legs, and has dark, thinning hair combed over the beginnings of a bald spot. He's freshly shaved, but with a few cuts. The other must be in his late thirties. He looks like a boxer: athletic, nose enthusiastically broken at some point, he's wearing a tight grey sweatshirt and equally tight jeans. His hair is short, thick and dark, like marmot fur. They each give a slightly sleazy grin as they greet us. They're very aware of the effect they have.

'Wow,' I say, 'do you always go around like that?'

'Saves time,' says the one in the suit.

'Be prepared,' says the other.

The suit man is called Pliquett, the boxer type is Lechner.

'How were things in the Acapulco yesterday?' asks Faller.

'Impressive,' says Pliquett.

'Well,' says Lechner, 'if I were one of those ladies, I'd never set foot on that stage again. But they're totally going through with it.'

'Do they know who you are?' I ask.

'No,' says Pliquett, 'we always stay incognito. But they know that there's someone there.'

'Did anyone catch your eye yesterday?' asks Faller.

'No,' says Lechner, 'the joint was practically empty, no one there but us and three guys from HSV, and they shut at ten. A Monday, though. The girls were walked home by plain-clothes officers, and everyone got in safely.'

Pliquett shrugs.

'When will you be there this evening?' I ask.

'From eight,' says Lechner.

'I might put in an appearance,' I say, 'so don't be surprised if you see me.'

'I've heard,' says Lechner, 'that you get itchy feet.'

'It has been known,' I say.

'I'll let you know if a job comes up with us,' he says.

'OK,' I say, 'then I'll see you later, gentlemen.'

Pliquett says: 'By all means.'

Faller and I set off to find Schulle and Brückner, and I'm glad that we're together. When I'm on my own, I regularly get lost in this star-shaped maze of a police station, every bloody corridor here looks the same, and you end up either going round in circles or walking into a wall.

'Will you come and have lunch with me?' Faller asks. 'I need to discuss something with you.'

'Me too. Sportbude?'

The Sportbude is a hot-dog stand near a football pitch right behind HQ. Our unofficial canteen. Unhealthy, but excellent.

'Sportbude,' he says.

Schulle and Brückner are sitting opposite each other at two desks, they've made their office feel like home with Scorsese film posters and maps of the city. Outside the window is Alsterdorf. Green parks, tall trees, terraced houses, suburban scenery.

Faller sits at the table where people normally sit for questioning, I lean against the filing cabinet because I don't like the interrogation table.

'How's it looking?' Faller asks.

'We've got the first responses on the four-by-fours,' says Schulle. 'Calabretta is coordinating that, thankfully, and he's out with the teams. Almost every car owner so far has an alibi for the time of the last murder, apart from a young woman in Eppendorf and an older man from Othmarschen who has mobility problems. But neither of them fits the footprints or our perpetrator profile.'

'What about the owner of the car whose number I gave you this morning?' I ask.

'Claudius Zandvoort,' says Schulle, 'yeah, he was at his theatre until two, the Okzidental. He's the artistic director there. And after that he was at home. His son confirmed that.'

'The Okzidental?' asks Faller. 'That's that old Kiez theatre, isn't it? So the guy would have been nearby at any rate.'

'Hmm,' I say, staring out of the window.

'Chas,' says Faller, 'is something wrong?'

'The alibi's not worth a damn,' I say. 'The son works as a junior lighting technician at his father's theatre, is completely dependent on him, and generally seems more like his underling. He'd confirm anything his father said.'

The three men in the room say nothing and look perplexedly at me.

'Do you know these people?' Faller asks.

I nod.

'Did you want to talk to me about it?' he persists.

I nod again.

'Yesterday evening, I was in the man's flat,' I say. 'We met at Carla's. But he started to creep me out. I got the feeling that something isn't right about him.'

'We ought to have the guy watched,' says Faller.

'Yes,' I say, 'he's tall, he's strong, he drives a Porsche Cayenne, and he's a total arsehole.'

'Good grief, Chas,' says Faller, 'what were you doing in the flat of somebody like that?'

'I don't know,' I say. I really don't know for the life of me.

'We'll have the chap watched right away,' he says. 'Schulle, will you take care of it?'

Schulle nods.

'And Brückner,' says Faller, 'have you been in touch with our sources? We really need a lead on Basso's murder.'

'Someone rang me this morning,' says Brückner. 'Apparently, Basso was trying to run a protection racket but wasn't getting anywhere. His death could certainly be linked to that. Even if he didn't land anything, he's bound to have seriously pissed a few people off.'

'And who should we talk to about that?' I ask. 'Did he have any hints for us?'

'Basso had a friend,' says Brückner, 'some bloke from the boxing scene. Wants to turn pro but it's not working out for him. Some people are saying he was in on the protection-money thing. But he's gone into hiding, nobody reckons they've seen him since the murder. Probably bricking it. Either over us, or over the people who've got Basso on their consciences. Heiner Matzen. Be good if we could scare him up.'

'Shall the two of us head over to St Pauli later?' I ask.

'Anytime,' says Brückner.

'OK,' I say, 'I'll bring along a little Kiez backup.'

Brückner isn't so sure.

STANDING UNDER A TREE, WEEPING

The Sportbude reeks of chip fat, so we wait for our food outside. The shish kebab's for Faller, the double portion of chips is for me.

'So,' says Faller, 'what's all this business with this Zandvoort? And why didn't I know anything about it?'

Swishing over his head is a red-and-white raffia umbrella.

'It was private,' I say. 'He chatted me up at Carla's and kind of flirted a bit with me. And for some reason I went along with it, at least at the start. But not for long.'

Our food arrives. I let my chips cool down a bit, Faller pushes his kebab off the stick.

'What kind of a chap is this Zandvoort then?' asks Faller.

'He's a bit like a clothed predator,' I say. 'He's very good-looking, but there's something furtive about him, nothing warm or nice. I don't know.'

I pop a chip in my mouth.

'To be honest, I wouldn't put much past him, but I somehow don't believe he'd get his hands dirty with messy murders. He'd be more the kind for a hired assassin.'

Wow, the chips are great.

'Are you still in touch with him?' Faller asks.

'No,' I say. 'But if you like, I'll meet up with him again and sound him out.'

Faller puts a piece of meat in his mouth. Around us, the wind rattles the trees.

'No,' he says, 'I don't think that should be you. I'll put Schulle on it.'

Now I almost feel a little sorry for Zandvoort. If you've got Schulle snapping at your heels, you're in for a hard time. Schulle's a terrier.

'What else?' he asks. 'How did it go yesterday morning? You wanted to go for a think, didn't you?'

'Right.'

'And? What does your head say?'

'He's gentle,' I say, 'he's sad, there's a hole in his soul and he's only trying to mend it. Nabbing him won't be dangerous.'

'None of that really fits with this Zandvoort,' says Faller.

'True,' I say. 'Doesn't fit him at all. Although...' Something dawns on me.

Shit, I'm so stupid it hurts.

'What?' asks Faller.

'John Zandvoort,' I say, pushing my chips away. 'I think I'm going to be sick.'

'John?' asks Faller. 'I thought he was called Claudius?'

'John's his adopted son,' I said, 'he's exactly what we're looking for. Damaged, disturbed, gentle, and sometimes exerts a huge force of attraction. And who says only Papa drives the Porsche?'

'You're not just dreaming all this up?' asks Faller.

'That's entirely possible,' I say. 'But when I see him, I feel like the snake and the rabbit at the same time.'

'We'll have him watched,' says Faller, 'better safe than sorry.'

'I'll get the guys to draw up an identikit picture,' I say. 'And maybe someone should call the State Crime Office in North-Rhine-Westphalia. The Zandvoorts lived in Aachen until six months ago. Claudius Zandvoort had a very decent job there, not the kind of thing you'd chuck in to work at a little theatre in the Kiez. There's something odd about the two of them moving to Hamburg. Something might have happened there.'

Faller nods and says, 'Interesting.'

'You wanted to tell me something too,' I say.

He wipes his face.

'Oh yes,' he says. 'Iron Siggi.'

'Faller,' I say.

'No, no,' he says, 'there's something lying dormant there, I swear it.'

'And why do you think that?'

'I've driven over there every day since Thursday,' says Faller, 'and so far, he hasn't reacted in any way. Doesn't even chuck me out. Seems totally indifferent to everything. Opens the door, lets me in without a word, then sits motionless in his armchair by the window and doesn't utter a syllable. I've tried everything – good God, I even took him cakes and beer. He's playing dead, not even looking at me. And we really do go back donkey's years.'

'That does sound weird,' I say, 'he always had people dancing to his tune, even in jail. Do you remember the time he bribed the warders and had some prostitutes smuggled in?'

'Oh yes,' says Faller. 'But the way he is now – you can't imagine it.'

'Is he ill?' I ask.

'I spoke to his doctor. He says he only saw him on Tuesday, and they were cracking jokes. I first went to see him on Thursday and found a wreck. And what happened in between?'

'A woman was murdered,' I say.

'Exactly,' says Faller. 'A girl who danced in the Kiez, and who apparently didn't know a soul in Hamburg apart from her flatmate, was killed.'

'But perhaps there was someone,' I say.

Faller nods.

'After all, we found his phone number in Margarete Sinckewicz's flat. Her funeral is on Thursday,' he says. 'I bet we'll see Siggi standing under a tree, weeping.'

'Geriatric love?' I ask.

Faller shrugs his shoulders and says, 'They say it happens, don't they?'

We go back to HQ. I take a detour to see the identikit specialists and have a picture of John made up for the team. Then Brückner and I drive to Sankt Pauli.

THE BOSS

Brückner parks at the Davidwache. The Reeperbahn is just the way it ought to be on a windy afternoon in March: swept clean. Barely any tourists, only a couple of guys outside a couple of sex shops, on the left, a band is carrying its instruments into the club where I guess they'll be playing later, standing on the right are two ageing streetwalkers, wearing down-at-heel heels, their greying hair still long and piled into ostentatious up-dos. They're chatting and you can tell by their eyes that they're talking about the old days.

'That's our man over there,' I say, pointing to Klatsche, who's hanging around by the crossroads.

He's wearing his leather jacket, same as ever, and as we come closer, he sticks his hands in his trouser pockets. Neither boy makes any move to shake hands politely.

'So,' says Brückner.

'*Moin*,' says Klatsche.

'Brückner,' I say, 'this is my neighbour Klatsche. Klatsche, this is my colleague Brückner.'

They nod to each other and nothing else happens.

Perhaps Brückner can smell that he's facing an ex-burglar-king here, and perhaps Klatsche still can't stand the smell of the law, apart from Faller and me, of course.

He takes me gently by the elbow.

'Hey,' I say, trying to keep it matter-of-fact. 'Thanks for taking the time.'

'Work fast, and home time comes sooner,' he says.

'What do you do?' asks Brückner.

Aha, a first step closer.

'I crack locks for money,' says Klatsche.

'He's the best in his field,' I say. 'And he knows everyone who's anyone in the Kiez.'

'OK,' says Brückner, 'so where do we start?'

'Who exactly are we looking for?' asks Klatsche.

'A friend of Basso's,' I say, 'a small-time boxer who's gone to ground.'

'Name?' asks Klatsche.

'Heiner Matzen,' I say.

'Let's go,' says Klatsche, walking off down the Reeperbahn.

'Whereabouts are we headed?' I ask.

'To the sun and freedom,' says Klatsche.

Inspector Brückner looks blankly at me.

'To the Grosse Freiheit,' I say.

'Aha.'

After about a hundred metres of Reeperbahn junk, we turn right. Klatsche stops halfway down the Freiheit, between two dives offering live sex every evening, and rings a bell beside a narrow door. Above the door is a sign advertising Thai Girls, but it belongs to the shop on the left.

A woman's voice comes from the intercom.

'Hello, what is it?'

'Julchen, it's Klatsche.'

There's a buzz and the door opens.

We follow Klatsche up the narrow stairs to the third floor. The walls are lined with the same red carpet as the steps, it's like walking through dark clouds.

'Cosy,' I say.

'People've hung out here for years,' says Klatsche with a grin. Then we arrive.

There's a tiny sofa by the window. The woman on the sofa must be Julchen. She's maybe four foot eleven and must weigh easily two hundredweight. She has bleached, pale-blonde hair in a kind of Monroe style. Her pink dress is ready to go out clubbing, but her feet are encased in stay-at-home brown slippers. Slices of cigarette smoke waft through the room. Opening the window is clearly strictly prohibited. Sitting in a colourful mismatch of armchairs are old men, middle-aged men and young men, they look tired and they're staring into the beer glasses in their hands. Standing behind the rancid bar is a girl of perhaps sixteen.

While Brückner and I hang around, somewhat awkwardly, in the doorway, Klatsche goes over to the little woman on the sofa. He bends down and kisses her on the brow.

'Hi, Julchen,' he says, 'how are you?'

'My feet hurt,' she says. Her voice sounds as young as a bell, it doesn't fit the woman at all. As if her voice had broken sometime, and been replaced.

Klatsche strokes her cheek in an affectionate-looking way.

Julchen glances over at us. 'Who've you brought with you?'

'They're OK,' he says. 'Friends of mine.'

'Hello,' I say. My colleague nods.

'Would your friends like a drink?'

'Would you like a drink?' asks Klatsche.

'A water would be nice,' says Brückner.

'There's only beer,' says Klatsche.

Julchen looks over to the young girl behind the bar and says: 'Three beers for the company.'

'Oh,' says Brückner, and then, once he has the beer in hand: 'Thanks.'

We sip at our beer, continue standing around in the doorframe like two bad pennies and say nothing.

'Why are you here?' asks Julchen.

Of course she's perfectly well aware that we're cops or similar. But she seems to trust that Klatsche won't bring trouble. He's still standing very close to her.

'Do you know where Heiner Matzen is?' he asks.

'Cigarette please,' says Julchen, holding out her right hand.

Klatsche takes a cigarette from his jacket, lights it and slips it between Julchen's fingers.

The woman kind of reminds me of a mafia godmother who got shrunk in the wash, but on a cycle with a heap of fabric conditioner. She smokes her fag to the end in three drags then throws out a general question: 'Anyone here know where Heiner Matzen's got to?'

As if on cue, everyone gets up, as if she's given an explicit order.

'Yeah, no, better be going,' says one.

'Uh-huh, me too, getting late,' says another.

'Bye then, Julchen, I'll call it a day,' says a third.

And so there's a comic little concert of melodies in the key of not-getting-involved-in-this, and in less than a minute, everyone but Julchen and us has left. Even the bargirl has slipped into the back room.

'Have a seat,' she says, pointing at the empty armchairs.

'Thanks,' I say, and she twists her little red lips into a fleeting smile that vanishes as quickly as it came.

Klatsche's pulled up an armchair to her sofa, he's holding her hand as if it's the most natural thing in the world, and she seems to like it.

'So, Heiner Matzen?'

Klatsche nods.

'What d'you want with the boy?'

'We just want to talk to him,' he says. 'Nothing's gonna happen to him.'

'About Basso, hm?'

'Exactly,' says Klatsche. 'What they did to him wasn't nice.'

'Noo,' she says, 'that wasn't nice at all.'

'Do you know anything?'

'From what I heard,' she says, raising her eyebrows, 'from what I heard, they were only supposed to take him on a little harbour tour. But, unfortunately, it turned into a big one.'

'Do you know anything about Basso's harbour tour?' asks Klatsche. 'Like who booked it?'

'God forbid,' she says. 'God forbid. And I really have no idea where Heiner's got to, but if I were you, I'd go and see Ali at the Blue Night.'

Bingo, I think.

'Thanks, Julchen,' says Klatsche.

'Be nice to Heiner,' she says, 'the little thumb-sucker's dying of fear at the moment.'

'Don't worry,' says Klatsche.

We put our beer down on the bar, Klatsche strokes Julchen's hair again and then we walk down the stairs and find ourselves back out on the Grosse Freiheit.

'So,' says Brückner, 'just who exactly was that, if you please?'

'That,' says Klatsche, 'was the boss.'

'I thought the boss was an Albanian,' says Brückner.

'Oh, him,' says Klatsche. 'He might own the joints, but our Jule here owns the people. She's the undisputed boss of all our spiritual welfare.'

'How come?' I ask.

'That's just the way it's always been,' he says. 'She sits up there and anyone who needs anything comes to her. But not for much longer I'm afraid.'

'What's up with her?' I ask.

'She's ill,' says Klatsche. 'If she's lucky, she'll live to see the summer.'

All three of us look up, past the houses, up to the heavens.

PROPER HARD FACES

The Blue Night is not much more than a sticky corner on Hans-Albers-Platz above a little club that used to be big in the nineties but where nobody goes these days. Nobody goes to the Blue Night either, because hardly anyone knows it's there. And if they do, they don't get in. Ali, the big, fat guy who runs the Blue Night, always puts a barstool in the doorway, and he himself sits near the barstool. He only pushes the stool aside for people he knows personally. Nobody knows where he earns his money because it can't come from the Blue Night. The beer and schnapps are cheap, and in any case, it's mainly his friends who drink here, and for them it's on the house. A policeman and a state prosecutor would never make it past Ali's barstool by themselves. But it's no problem for Klatsche.

We go up the five steps to the barstool, Klatsche leading the way. He sticks his head through the door and says: 'Ali, my old fish roll.'

The stool is tipped aside by a greasy mitt and we're in. I've never seen Ali before, only heard of him. I'm impressed. He's a good six foot three, his body is powerful, he's wearing jeans, a fine-checked shirt and a tweed jacket, his moustache is as bushy as you'd expect on a man from Izmir, and the rest of his dark hair is slicked back with a good dollop of styling cream. There's a heavy gold chain lying on his hairy chest.

'Hey, kid,' he says to Klatsche. His voice buzzes. He looks at me and Brückner. 'Afternoon, madam, sir.'

'Chastity Riley,' I say, 'State Prosecution Service. And this is my colleague, Brückner, of the CID.'

'Can I offer you a coffee?' asks Ali.

'Love one,' I say.

'Do have a seat,' he says, with a chivalrous wave at a group of armchairs in the far corner, then vanishes behind the bar and fiddles with a filter-coffee machine. The ceiling is bedecked with old boxing gloves and colourful football scarves representing every European league, my boots make a sticky sound as I walk towards the table he's offered us. We lower ourselves onto the deep bench seats. I avoid touching the tabletop. There are chains of lights on the walls between posters and photographs. Ali with famous footballers, Ali with famous trainers, Ali with shady agents, Ali with infamous boxers. The TV behind our backs is showing porn. Barely any daylight pierces the windows, the stained glass is sticky and dusty. I imagine that a load of beer goes flying here every evening.

Klatsche looks at me, eyebrows raised, and I think he's trying to play footsie with me under the table. At least I hope it's him and not Brückner. But Brückner is looking about as sticky as the room, and I'd say he isn't in the mood for footsie right now.

Ali returns with a tray, on which are four cups of coffee, along with cream instead of milk and sweetener instead of sugar. The coffee is so bitter and stewed that it hits me like a punch in the face. Ali is breathing heavily as he joins us at the table.

'We've just been to see Julchen,' says Klatsche, 'and she reckoned we should pop in here because you might be able to help us.'

'Julchen, uh-huh,' says Ali, leaning back and drinking coffee. If we want anything, we'll have to ask.

'Is Heiner Matzen here, by any chance?' I ask.

'Ha!' says Ali, and Brückner jumps a little.

'Is he?' I ask.

'What do you want with him?' asks Ali.

'Just a chat,' says Brückner.

Ali looks at Klatsche.

'They just want a chat,' says Klatsche, 'honest.'

'Anyone going to find out about this?' asks Ali.

'No,' I say, 'we weren't here.'

'The boy's under my protection and he's done nothing wrong. He's such small fry that nobody even sees him. If any harm comes to him after he's spoken to you, you'll never set foot in here again.'

Well, that's clear.

'Nothing will happen to him,' I say, 'you have my word.'

'OK,' says Ali, standing up. He goes to the bar. Behind the bar, there's a door, Ali pulls a key from his trouser pocket and unlocks the door.

'Come here a moment.'

Heiner Matzen is about Klatsche's age and has a round head. His small bull neck is perfectly shaved, his eyes flit to and fro, and he looks like he's borrowed his front teeth from a rabbit. He's wearing a thick sweatshirt, baggy joggers and bright trainers. When he sees us, he takes a step back and looks at Ali in desperation.

'Who's this?'

'They just want to talk to you,' says Ali.

'But I don't want to talk to anyone,' says Heiner.

Klatsche glances at me, we stand up and approach the man. He takes another step back.

'Heiner,' says Klatsche, 'we're looking for the people who killed your friend. They ought to do time for that.'

'If they find out that I spoke to you, you can book me a space in the freezer right away.'

'They won't find out,' I say. 'We were never here, promise.'

'I'll be screwed on the Kiez if I grass,' he says, 'who'll work with me then?'

'How are you going to work at all if there are two guys running around, out to get you?'

That was Brückner, intervening from his bench in the corner, and he said exactly the right thing.

Heiner looks at Ali.

'Go on,' the older man says, 'those arseholes murdered your mate.'

Heiner breathes in and out again.

'OK. Let's talk.'

Ali pulls him out of the doorway to his den and puts an

arm around his shoulders. Klatsche and I walk back around the bar and sit on two stools, Brückner comes cautiously closer and stands behind us.

'Spill,' says Ali.

'Basso was trying to get in on protection,' says Heiner.

'We know that,' I say. 'But it wasn't going so well, was it?'

Heiner shakes his head and pinches his lips together.

'He'd just had it up to here with being the little idiot that nobody takes seriously. He wanted to get some serious dough in his pockets for once.'

'What about you?' I ask.

'I want to box professionally,' he says, 'I want people to respect me.'

'Respect, huh?' says Klatsche.

'Yeah,' he says. 'If people don't respect you, your arse is cooked.'

'So whose toes did Basso step on with his protection-racket thing?' asks Brückner.

'Ah,' says Heiner, 'didn't even get that far. He'd walk in somewhere and say his bit and they wouldn't even listen to him. I told him from the start there was no point. You gotta look brutal for that shit.'

'Basso looked like a hairdresser,' says Klatsche.

'D'you know him?' asks Heiner.

'A bit,' says Klatsche.

'He was a good guy, seriously,' says Heiner.

'Why did Basso have visitors on Wednesday evening?' I ask. 'In your opinion?'

'He did something dumb,' says Heiner. 'Tried something and got way out of his depth. Tried to blackmail some guy.'

'Who?' I ask.

'Not a clue,' says Heiner, 'but he said it was someone with money and a reputation to lose. Some old fogey.'

'What did he want to blackmail him over?' asks Brückner.

'He wasn't saying,' says Heiner, 'all he said was that he knew something that could seriously harm this guy, could finish him. Basso went round to the guy's place three times on Wednesday, wanted to seriously piss him off about it.'

'So they knew each other,' I say.

'Yeah,' says Heiner, 'someone from the Kiez. But I don't know for sure. He said he didn't want to drag me into it.'

'When did you last see Basso?' I ask.

'Wednesday evening,' he says, 'around eleven.'

I look at Brückner. 'He was already dead by then, wasn't he?'

Brückner nods.

'Yes,' says Heiner, 'he was already dead.'

Ali hugs him tighter.

'He called me around eight,' says Heiner, 'he was fucking angry, ranting and swearing, said the guy was digging his heels in and saying no way was he paying, and that he'd threatened to send some guys round. Basso said he wasn't gonna let anyone fuck with him and that he'd make his info public. The guy needed to know who he was dealing with. Everyone did.'

'And then?' I ask.

'He said to pick him up at ten, to drive him down to the port 'cos he was meeting someone there.'

Me, I think.

He looks at his feet.

'I keep telling myself,' he says, 'that if I'd picked him up sooner, the wankers wouldn't have got him. But I didn't get to his place till nearly half-ten, I was running kind of late. I called him and hung up right away. That was always our signal for him to come down, he didn't have a doorbell, he lived in that office place. When he hadn't come down by quarter to, I rang again. He didn't answer. I was just getting out of my car 'cos I'd got scared, when these guys came out of the building.'

'What guys?' I ask.

'Two big guys,' he says, 'they were talking but I didn't understand them, I think they were Russian. They had proper hard faces and shaved heads, and I'm like almost certain it was Russian they were talking. Or something like that.'

'Can you describe them in more detail?' asks Brückner, whipping out his notebook.

'They were about thirty maybe, both way over six foot. Wearing black bomber jackets and black steel-capped boots. They got into a car, some kind of dark van. Could've been brown, or blue maybe, I couldn't really see, it was dark.'

'Registration?' asks Brückner.

Heiner shakes his head.

'But then I went up to his flat. All I saw at first was his door open, and then there was Basso, lying there.'

'Did you touch anything?' I ask.

Heiner shrugs. 'I might have slammed the door as I ran out, but I don't know. I was so scared, man.'

'The boy came to me in the middle of the night,' says Ali, 'like he'd been through a mincer.'

He looks at us. 'OK, that's enough now, folks. Everybody out of here.'

Heiner looks at him wide-eyed.

'Not you, obviously,' says Ali, 'you stay nice and safe with me right here till those arseholes are off the streets.'

'Thank you, Heiner,' I say, 'thanks.'

'You're welcome,' he says. 'Will you let me know when you've got them?'

'Will do,' says Klatsche.

I give Ali my card.

'Just in case.'

When we step outside, it's raining.

FOR SECURITY REASONS

Outside, twilight is settling over the city. I'm lying in the bathtub and Klatsche's trying to fit an extra lock to my door. But it's not going to plan and he's swearing.

'Leave it,' I say, letting a little lather drop from my hand into the bath. 'It's not that big a deal.'

'It is that big a deal,' he says. 'I don't want you to get hurt.'

'I won't get hurt,' I say.

'Shut it,' he says, 'darling.'

Darling. Oh right. I submerge myself and emerge again, get out of the bath, dry myself, pull on my dressing gown and go to check on the workman.

'I'm going out again later,' I say. 'Want to come?'

'As far as I'm concerned, we could stay here,' he says, tugging at my towelling belt.

'Hey,' I say.

'Hey yourself,' he says, putting his tools away and grabbing me round the waist.

'I'm going to the Acapulco tonight,' I say. 'You know, the club where the dead girls danced. Want to come too, or not?'

'Course I'm coming.'

'I don't need protection though,' I say.

'What do you need then?' he asks, and at the exact moment that we decide to let the lock look after itself, my phone rings. It's Calabretta, calling from HQ.

Shit. Just when you've got yourself a private life for once.

'Let go,' I tell Klatsche, pulling at my bathrobe. 'I have to take this.'

He sighs and lets go, and I take it.

'What's up?'

'I called Aachen,' Calabretta says. 'Faller says you had a kind of suspicion.'

'Yes,' I say, 'I did. And?'

'They had a weird case there about six months ago,' he says. 'They found a girl from a touring ballet company in a public toilet. Someone had shaved her hair and she'd been strangled, but the perpetrator let her go before it was too late. And he gave her sedatives, so she couldn't remember a thing. They never caught the guy.'

'What were the pills?' I ask.

'Phenobarbital,' he says.

'John Zandvoort,' I say, and need a little support from the wall.

'We're keeping an eye on him from pretty much right now,' says Calabretta. 'He's not taking a single step without us.'

THE USUAL NIGHT-TIME EXTRAS

It's just after eleven as we walk up the Grosse Freiheit. Klatsche has his arm round my shoulders: you might think we're just a couple out for an evening stroll.

'Let's run up some expenses,' says Klatsche, pushing open the door to the Acapulco. The two heavy bouncers watch us, piqued.

Couples are something of a rarity here.

The place looks very different this evening from the other afternoon. Like it's got dressed up for a night out. The light is pink and yellow and soft, there are disco balls spinning all over the ceiling, the dark-velvet upholstered chairs are acting comfy, and the bar is gleaming at its full width.

Sitting at a table to the front left is Pliquett, in his blue suit; Lechner is lounging in a chair somewhere in the middle. There are about ten other punters here. On the stage, a blonde girl in red lingerie is lying on a turntable, doing the splits in complicated ways. The loudspeakers are blaring out a bizarre rock version of 'Fever'. We sit at a small table at the back of the room. A woman comes towards us with nothing on up top. Down below, she's wearing a tiny white apron – well, really, it's more of a lacy belt.

'You have to buy a drink to sit here,' she says. 'What can I get you?'

'Two Fantas please,' says Klatsche.

We both know that we might need a clear head tonight.

She turns away without another word.

'Pretty things,' I say.

'The older I get,' says Klatsche, 'the less pretty I find boob jobs.'

'Don't talk to me about getting old,' I say, 'or I'll call Faller and have you arrested.'

The nude waitress returns. She has our drinks with her. Two Fantas have never looked more boring. The glasses are small and the stuff is so flat that there's not even the idea of carbon dioxide left in there.

'That'll be twenty-two euros,' she says.

Klatsche raises his eyebrows, I lay the money on the table then look around a bit. The men in the Acapulco couldn't be more varied. There's everything from the 'chic industrial designer' to the insecure uncle. To our left, to my shock, there's a man who looks like my former gynaecologist, but thank God it isn't him.

'Ah,' says Klatsche, 'a new audience.'

Two tables over, a group of Asian businessmen are settling down. They're all wearing the same dark suits and the same glasses. One of them doesn't have glasses, he has a bald spot instead, and he could as easily be the boss as the idiot of the group. The waitress goes to their table and at once joy is unconfined. They order a beer and a schnapps for each of them, and a bottle of bubbly for the table. I don't even want to imagine what these boys will have clocked up by the end of the night.

'It's like Grand Central Station in here,' says Klatsche, nodding at the door. Someone else is coming in. A thin young man with short brown hair, I have to pull myself together, stop myself keeling over, and I slip down a little deeper into my chair. It's John. He's here.

Ten seconds later, the door opens again and two middle-aged men in dark jackets walk into the joint. They must be the police.

My God. It's happening.

'That's him,' I say.

'That's who?' asks Klatsche.

'That's the guy we're here for,' I say, noticing the way the cold sweat runs down my back.

'Holy shit,' says Klatsche, reaching under the table for my hand.

I watch John. He walks past Lechner to the front and sits down by the stage. To his left, at the other end of the row, is Pliquett. I notice that Lechner reacts to John at once, immediately has an eye on him. The back of my neck tenses. The two cops who followed John through the door stay in the background. They've settled themselves at the bar and exchanged glances with Lechner and Pliquett. The four men are on professional alert.

I take a swig of my Fanta after all. It tastes hideous.

John orders a drink. The topless woman seems to leave him completely cold, he's staring at the stage. Then there's a change of personnel. The blonde girl jumps off her turntable, which disappears into the floor. A redhead takes to the pole. She's wearing black underwear and isn't bad at her stuff, somehow keeps one leg permanently straight up in the air, her long curls whip around her shoulders with every movement, while Whitney Houston sings about Saving All Her Love. The Far Eastern gentlemen love it. Five minutes later, she's back down from the stage. John sits very calmly on his chair. He seems older and harder now, he doesn't seem as defenceless and desperate as usual. I'm almost shitting myself with fear.

Klatsche stares into the middle distance, but he's still holding my hand under the table.

Quarter of an hour later, the redhaired dancer who was up on the stage just now has taken her make-up off. She's plaited up her hair, she's wearing jeans and a pink jumper, classic Kiez working-girl look. She walks past us, has a quick chat with the open-air waitress and leaves the Acapulco.

And then John stands up and walks after her. Lechner darts a quick look at Pliquett, then his colleagues at the bar, and all four of them nod to each other. Lechner waits a moment, for John to be out of the door, then he stands up and paces gently outside.

'OK,' I say to Klatsche, 'it's on. We're out of here.'

We leave the Acapulco at almost the same moment as my colleagues who were standing at the bar. Lechner is standing outside the door. 'Ms Riley,' he says.

'Can we tag along?' I ask.

'If you like,' he says, 'and if you do as I say.'

I nod and we introduce ourselves to the others.

'Lotter,' says one, 'evening.'

'Kurbjuweit,' says the other.

Total pros.

'OK,' says Lechner, 'we'll split up and go for a stroll in small groups.'

The redhaired dancer is walking up the Freiheit, John following her two metres behind, Lechner keeping three metres behind him, Klatsche and I try to keep at an inconspicuous five-metre distance, reinforcements at our backs in the shape of Lotter and Kurbjuweit. At the end of the Freiheit, our dark procession turns left, we walk up the Reeperbahn, the dancer out at the front, John always close behind her. I sense how nervous Klatsche is. I feel dizzy, I'm gripping his arm.

'Are you OK?' he asks.

'Yes, course,' I say.

No, I think.

On the corner of the Hamburger Berg, John catches up with the dancer and speaks to her. Lechner saunters past at a distance, looking in the sex-shop windows, we stop, Lotter and Kurbjuweit walk past slowly on our left, eyeing up a group of girls. I see John talking to the dancer. She smiles at him, then she laughs. Everything looks totally safe, and she seems so unsuspecting. But, to be honest: *I'd* let him talk to me, and I never let anyone talk to me.

I wish I knew what he's saying, by the look on her face it must be something amusing, charming. She's laughing again, and she puts her hand on his forearm. They almost look like an item, like they're old friends. If the five of us weren't after them, you could think everything was perfectly normal. They start moving again, they're talking and walking side by side, and they turn off down Hamburger Berg, there's nightlife here even on a Tuesday evening, there's one pub after another, it's always buzzing with life here, everyone can do whatever they like here, and for as long as they like it.

It's weirdly quiet in my head, as if all the sounds around me have been cut out. I feel like I'm walking through a soap bubble, I can only hear my own breath, all I can see clearly is John and the dancer ahead of me, everything else is in the mist, out of focus.

As he walks, Lechner turns back to us for a moment, looks at me, raises his eyebrows and makes the international hand gesture for telephone. I assume he doesn't want me to call him, that he wants me to call for backup from the police. I nod, pull my own phone out of my coat pocket and ring Calabretta.

'*Pronto?*'

'Are you on duty?' I ask.

'Of course,' he says.

'We're out in the Kiez,' I say, 'tailing John Zandvoort. Will you call Brückner and Schulle? I think we're going to need them any moment.'

'No problem,' he says, 'I'll let them know.'

I hang up and take Klatsche's hand again. Halfway up the street, John and the dancer stop outside a bar. It's the Sorgenbrecher, a Kiez pub with an ancient soul, I like it a lot, and I'm almost outraged that the young woman could be in danger if she walks in there. John holds the door for her, they go in. Lechner squeezes into the doorway over the road, rolls a cigarette and waits for Klatsche and me to join him. His face looks hard and grey.

'I'll go in there and keep an eye on the young woman,' he says. 'Will you two stay out here please and watch the door? If they leave the joint, we'll follow them in the same formation as before. And in that case, you'll need to give your people our approximate direction.'

Behind us, Lotter and Kurbjuweit are strolling up and down.

'Think we're on the right track?' I ask.

'Let's just pray that we are,' he says, 'and that some other man isn't about to stroll into the Acapulco and blow our theory to smithereens.'

'Pliquett's still there, he's got things under control,' I say, 'and you don't have to carry the entire responsibility for this. I'm here too, so that's a total of four shoulders. OK? We'll wait here until they come out again.'

Lechner nods and disappears into the Sorgenbrecher.

Klatsche and I position ourselves in the doorway and I make an effort to breathe evenly. Klatsche doesn't say a word and I squeeze his hand a bit harder, he squeezes back, we glance at each other, and somehow, it's going to be all right.

We wait about half an hour. Just after midnight, John and the dancer leave the bar. She seems relaxed and a touch tiddly, so does he, they seem to be getting on like a house on fire. They walk back up the Hamburger Berg, towards the Reeperbahn, Lechner emerges from the pub, we nod to each other, Lotter and Kurbjuweit broaden their shoulders and together we stick to John and the girl's heels. They cross the Reeperbahn, run over the four-lane road like teenagers. Once we're on the other side, I call Calabretta.

'On our way to Sankt Pauli in two cars,' he says, 'approximate direction?'

'South of the Reeperbahn,' I say, 'towards the Silbersack.'

'OK,' he says, 'we're very close then.'

John and the girl walk up Silbersackstrasse, towards Hein-Köllisch-Platz. Almost an island of peace amid the partying. The little restaurants and cafés are extremely civilised by Kiez standards, the Japanese cherry trees form an elegant circle around the square, just waiting for their moment – soon they'll be able to throw their blossom into the ring. It's very quiet; at this time of night, there's almost nobody around here. From now on, we have to be very careful.

Lechner shows us the way: John and the dancer walk

down the middle of the square, towards the Elbe, he follows at a twenty-metre distance, keeping to one side, Klatsche and I keep another ten metres behind, Lotter and Kurbjuweit drop back. John and the girl are on Antonistrasse now, a bit of a squeeze, hard to spread out there. Lechner reels slightly, playing the drunkard. We act all lovey-dovey, sitting on a bench.

The usual night-time extras.

There's no sign of Lotter and Kurbjuweit now. I hope they're still there.

There's a view of the port from the end of Antonistrasse, the moon has suddenly broken through the clouds, switching on a light that's rather too bright for our liking. It reveals a traffic island, an area of artificial lawn, a few plastic palm trees, the pedestrian bridge to the fish market and, on the left, the block where Zandvoort lives, where John has the loft apartment. Every window in the glass-and-steel building is dark, nobody home. And John's about to take the dancer into that self-same building. They're heading for the door.

All the way here, I'd been hoping it would all just fizzle out. That they'd stroll a bit further, maybe have another nightcap in some bar, and then say goodbye. That she'd turn and wave, that he'd wave back, and bye, nice to meet you.

I stare at the back of her head, which is about thirty metres from me, and think: beat it. Just beat it. Run away.

As if I could turn this thing around.

I've got a growing sense that we're using her, it's not a good feeling. And she isn't acting the least bit like a hard-bitten honey trap. Dammit, she must know who she might be going home with. But he probably seems so harmless and so nice that she's totally forgotten what else he might be.

I wish I could scream. Stop, wait, cut, curtain. I'd just have to fire off a single scream and this whole shitshow would be over. We've got tyre tracks, we've got DNA, and if it's John's, it's enough. But of course I know that taking him like this would be way, way better. Then there'll be nothing more to interpret and everything will be over by the morning.

I'm so sorry for him.

It's insane, but I'm just so very sorry for him.

Lechner starts to stagger, he drops onto the little traffic island in the grass and belches. John and the girl spot him, she giggles. Klatsche and I vanish into the doorway opposite for a pretend snog. John's got to the door with the girl now. He unlocks it, they walk in. I can hardly breathe, and I think my heart misses a beat. Lechner hastily gathers himself up and sprints to the door but doesn't catch it before it shuts.

'Shit,' he says.

We flit over to him, I'm trying hard to remember to breathe, Klatsche pulls his skeleton key from his jacket pocket.

'Hey,' says Lechner, 'why didn't you say you had that thing before?'

Klatsche looks at me. 'Shall I?'

'Wait,' I hear myself say, 'let's give him five minutes.'

Fuck, I think.

'No more though. Ten could be too long,' says Lechner.

'I know,' I say as I phone Calabretta.

Stay cool.

Just stay cool.

DEVOTIONAL OBJECTS

Three minutes later, Calabretta, Brückner and Schulle climb out of two dark-blue saloon cars. Lotter and Kurbjuweit emerge from the darkness.

'OK,' I say, 'we're going in.'

Lechner and Calabretta stay below, guarding the door, Lotter and Kurbjuweit keep an eye on the building from the other side of the street, Brückner, Schulle, Klatsche and I take the lift up to the fifth floor, where we creep past Zandvoort's door and up the stairs to John's attic flat.

Klatsche pulls out his lock pick again and when the CID guys nod and undo the safety catches on their guns, he gets to work. I cling to the wall beside the door. Let's not kid ourselves: I don't want to go in there.

Then there's a click, someone screams, it's the dancer, then voices – Brückner and Schulle – it's mayhem, everything is happening very fast, and then it goes almost quiet again, there's just a quiet whimpering still echoing in the stairwell. I inhale and exhale and step through the door. The dancer is sitting stock still on the sofa by the window. Her eyes are wide, Klatsche is sitting beside her with his hand on her back.

John's standing with his hands up, face to the wall, Brückner has him covered, Schulle is searching him. John is quivering, and he's crying. I look around the flat. A room with a window. Apart from the sofa, there's a table with two chairs, standing on a sideboard are two glasses, a bottle of gin and a bottle of tonic. In the far corner of the room there's a tall, narrow cupboard.

Schulle reaches into John's trouser pockets. He pulls two sturdy cable ties from the left and a packet of pills from the right. The cardboard box is labelled: phenobarbital.

'OK,' Schulle says.

He explains John's rights to him, pulls his hands onto his back and handcuffs him.

John keeps his eyes shut and doesn't make another sound. It's almost like he's not even there.

Brückner lowers his gun.

Then they take him away.

I call Faller first, then the SOCO guys. Klatsche is still sitting with the dancer on the sofa, he still has his hand on her back. She's staring into space, moving her upper body forward and back, again and again, forward, back. She seems to be slowly realising that she's been lucky.

I sit down beside her. I feel sick.

'It's over,' says Klatsche, 'it's over.'

I'm not sure exactly who he's telling, her or me. I hear Calabretta and Lechner running up the stairs. Calabretta stops in the doorway for a moment and looks at the room. Lechner comes over to us.

'Should I take the young lady back to the station?'

'No,' I say, 'it's OK. We'll get a female officer to drive her home. Can you arrange that?'

Lechner nods, pulls out his phone and makes a call.

The dancer looks at him.

'You were there this evening, weren't you?' she asks, once he's hung up.

'Yes,' he says.

'I knew it wasn't you,' she says with a smile. 'But I'd never have thought that that guy just now, that he, oh man, he was so nice, I really never clicked, I'd have bet on it being that sleazy businessman in the front row.'

Poor Pliquett, better keep that one between us.

'Just goes to show,' says Lechner, 'very few things in life are the way they seem.'

He says goodbye, and, ten minutes later, a woman from the vice squad comes to give the dancer a lift. She's used to caring for these pretty nightlife creatures, she'll do a good job.

'We ought to have a look in that cupboard over there in the corner,' I say, once the two women have left.

'Yes,' says Calabretta, 'we probably ought. Are you thinking what I'm thinking?'

I nod.

We go over to the narrow thing. Calabretta tries to open it. It's locked.

'Klatsche,' I say, 'would you please...?'

Klatsche looks crumpled and truly exhausted. He stands

up from the sofa, comes over to us, pulls his skeleton key from his jacket pocket and inserts it.

'Are you ready?' he asks.

I nod, but cling to my colleague – discreetly though, hoping that he doesn't notice. There's a click and Klatsche takes a step to the side. Calabretta opens the cupboard doors. I put my hand to my face, a powerful smell wafts towards us, sweet and sad.

Lying on the upper shelf are four carpet knives. Three are blood-encrusted. The fourth is gleaming and looks unused. Lying to its right is a green, short-haired wig. On the bottom shelf are three pairs of jeans, three jumpers, three jackets, three sets of underwear – all meticulously folded – and three pairs of shoes. Lying on the cupboard floor is crumpled, blood-smeared plastic sheeting. And on the middle shelf, stuck to the back wall of the cupboard, between the shelves above and below it, is a picture. It's a portrait of a woman. She's in her mid-thirties, she's very pretty, her thick, dark hair falls softly around her face, she's smiling tenderly at the camera. Tacked above the photo are three scalps, making it almost a kind of sculpture, an altar with gruesome devotional objects.

'Holy shit,' says Calabretta.

She came to
pick me up from school
just like every day
it was a beautiful day
it was summer we were
strapped in
she drove fast
she always drove fast
she looked over to me
she smiled
she squinted
she often squinted but
only a bit she didn't
see the lorry
so she just
drove into it
the thing
on the lorry just
sliced off her head
above her eyes
I saw it
then I had to
stay with him or
he wouldn't get the money
he said

he had to take tablets
to stop the fits
sometimes I took
one of the tablets
the tablets
are good
you
get
very
calm
I'm not
a good son
he always says so
but
I worked
in his theatre I was
always honest
I always did what
he wanted
but the girls
the beautiful girls in that
filthy shithole they
danced there
but they didn't belong there
it wasn't good
for them no one
noticed them
but I

saw them saw
how beautiful they are
they were with me
they didn't run away
nobody took them away
they were perfect perfect perfect I wish
you could've seen them
Mama

BUSINESS ON BROADWAY

In my Prosecution Service office, at my desk with a cup of coffee. It's nine a.m., the sky is overcast but there's a pale-pink shimmer over the city. An hour ago, someone called from police HQ to tell me that John hanged himself in his cell last night. He put his bedsheet around his neck and strung himself up from the window bars.

We spent the whole of yesterday trying to get anything at all out of him, Mr Borger was with him round the clock. Nothing. The only thing, and he kept talking about her, was his dead mother. Not a word about the dancers. Mr Borger says it's perfectly possible that John didn't even know what he'd done, and that if he did, he probably didn't realise how gruesome it was. We just spoke on the phone again, Mr Borger and I, and he's reproaching himself. He says he should have guessed that John was a suicide risk. He says the boy must have felt endlessly lonely and lost. He says he'd like to speak to Zandvoort. He suspects that he could give us a few answers. Apparently, Zandvoort's meant to be coming into the HQ this afternoon.

When my police colleagues finally got him on the phone

on Wednesday morning, to tell him that his son had killed three women, he was in ... wait for it ... New York. He'd flown out on Tuesday, said he had business on Broadway. He was planning to get the next plane back and then come straight over here.

I'm looking forward to his appearance.

DARNING SOCKS

'Hello,' says Faller.

'Hello,' I say.

'*I'm Johnny Cash*,' he says in English.

I have to laugh.

'Cut the crap, please,' I say. 'Is Zandvoort here?'

Faller leans against his desk and smokes a Roth-Händle. Lying in front of him are today's papers. 'Scalp Killer Caught', they say. 'Sankt Pauli Breathes Again', they claim. 'At the Eleventh Hour: Monster Had His Fourth Victim Lined Up'.

'He should show up any moment,' he says, 'he said something about eleven.'

'And then?' I ask.

'Then Calabretta and I will give him a good going-over,' he says. 'You and Mr Borger are welcome to watch. Maybe he'll have something to tell us that could interest our colleagues in Aachen. I get the feeling that we might nail him as an accessory after the fact.'

'Is the mirror room free?' I ask.

'We've got it booked,' says Faller.

'Does Zandvoort know that John hanged himself?'

'I told him an hour ago, while he was still at the airport.'

'And?'

'Didn't seem to bother him all that much. I got the impression that it didn't even surprise him. I mean, if the police called me to tell me that my son—'

'Adopted son,' I say.

'Does that make a difference?'

'Clearly it does for Zandvoort,' I say.

Faller says nothing and wipes his face with his hands. I walk around his desk and let myself drop into his chair.

'How are you doing, anyway?'

'All right,' he says. 'I was so relieved yesterday not to have been there in the night. That makes me think.'

'Do you want to retire?'

He drags on his cigarette and looks at me. He looks done in, really knackered. The longer he goes without speaking, the more uneasy I feel. I can't imagine this place without him. But I also realise how urgently he needs rest and peace. I gulp.

'Perhaps,' he says, 'the boys on the burglary squad could use an old hand.'

'Bollocks,' I say, 'you might just as well sit there darning socks.'

Faller grins at me, then his black office phone rings.

'Hello?'

He takes one last drag on his cigarette and stubs it out.

'Excellent,' he says, 'thanks.'

'Is he here?'

'Just come in through the gate,' he says. 'Let's go.'

He walks to the door.

'I'll be with you in five minutes,' I say, waiting for Mr Borger and trying not to think about what will happen when the day comes when my old colleague isn't there anymore.

BEHIND THE WALL

It's like all Zandvoort's attractiveness has been blown away. There's nothing left of that disquieting allure that he exerted on me just a few days ago. I don't even find him good-looking now. I don't know if that's to do with his bizarre carryings-on on Monday, or the fact that I'm now certain that he knew. He knew what his son was doing, and he didn't stop him, possibly because he just didn't care.

And somehow, all that is linked to the death of Basso.

Zandvoort is sitting on one side of the table in the interview room, Calabretta is sitting on the other, standing in the middle of the table is a voice recorder. Faller is leaning on the wall to the left of Zandvoort, who has on a dark-grey suit, a grey shirt and a hard twist to his lips. He looks leaden. There's no sign of life in him.

'What a granite face,' says Mr Borger. We're standing behind the soundproof, mirrored windowpane that looks onto the interview room.

'Yes,' I say, 'he can be seriously terrifying.'

I press the button in front of me so we can hear what they're saying.

'And you never noticed,' says Calabretta, 'that your son might have a ... shall we call it a somewhat peculiar attitude towards women?'

'He didn't say much,' says Zandvoort, leaning back, at his ease.

'Did he have a girlfriend?' asks Calabretta.

'No,' says Zandvoort, 'he was an idiot, a late starter in every respect.'

He subjects his fingernails to an inspection.

'John had no get up and go.'

'You don't seem particularly concerned that he killed three women,' says Calabretta. 'And you don't seem particularly concerned that he is now dead.'

'We didn't have a very good relationship,' says Zandvoort. 'After his mother's death, I felt obliged to take him in, but I soon realised that that was a mistake. To be honest, I'm not all that sorry to be rid of him.'

Faller shakes his head.

'And you insist that you heard and saw nothing in relation to the murders of these girls?' asks Calabretta.

'I'm very tired when I get in from the theatre at night,' says Zandvoort. 'I generally go straight to bed and sleep deeply.'

'Your adopted son killed the women upstairs from you, he hoarded the women's scalps in his flat,' says Faller. 'And you seriously claim to have picked nothing up about it?'

Calabretta stands up, he and Faller change places.

'The last time I entered John's apartment,' says Zandvoort, 'was when we moved in six months ago.'

'You really didn't have much time for the boy, hm?' asks Faller.

'I said as much earlier,' says Zandvoort.

He's so callous that I'd like to spit on the glass.

'Forensics had a good look at your Porsche yesterday,' says Faller. 'John used it to transport the dead women to the Elbe. I suppose you didn't notice that either.'

'I barely use the car,' says Zandvoort. 'I last drove it a good two months ago. I prefer to take a taxi, I like to have someone else drive me.'

Calabretta stands up and walks up and down by the side wall. I can see that he's on the brink of flipping out. He hates guys with big mouths.

'Are you familiar with the drug phenobarbital?' asks Faller.

'Yes,' says Zandvoort. 'I've been taking it for almost twenty years. I suffer from a mild form of epilepsy. It runs in my family. After my wife's accident, I was under a lot of stress and it was diagnosed then. The meds help me live with it very well.'

'John used phenobarbital to sedate the women before he killed them,' says Faller.

'The stuff is freely accessible in my bathroom. I presume he just helped himself,' says Zandvoort.

'And you never noticed that there was any missing?' asks Faller.

'No, I didn't notice.'

I can see that Faller doesn't believe a word of it.

'What do you make of him, Mr Borger?' I ask.

'The man's a psychopath,' he says. 'He seems utterly lacking in empathy. I haven't seen anything like it for a long time.'

My mobile rings. It's Brückner. I leave the room for a moment.

'We've got two Russians here,' he says, 'they're a pretty good fit for the picture Heiner Matzen painted of the blokes he saw outside Basso's place.'

'Where'd you pick them up?' I ask.

'Lechner and Pliquett spotted them in some pub yesterday,' says Brückner. 'Apparently throwing money around, and then, in the early hours, they went and dossed down in a brown van. We ran a routine check on the van this morning and found the gentlemen along with a whole crate of blunt instruments.'

'Interesting,' I say.

'We're keeping the two of them here for the moment,' he says.

'You should pop round to Ali's and convince Heiner Matzen to take part in an identity parade,' I say, 'the room here will be free in a bit. I could book it out again.'

'I'm on my way,' says Brückner.

I hang up and go back in to Mr Borger.

'Well?' I ask.

'He's starting to stir,' says Mr Borger.

Zandvoort is still sitting at the table but he seems a little smaller than before. Faller is leaning back casually in his chair, Calabretta is standing at the side of the table, resting his arms on the top of it.

'I think,' says Mr Borger, 'the lads have just grabbed him by the balls.'

'So what exactly happened in Aachen?' asks Calabretta. 'You had it good there.'

Zandvoort doesn't answer.

'Was there really any need,' says Faller, 'to move to Hamburg so hastily? To take a job that's not a whit better than the one in Aachen?'

Zandvoort rubs his forehead.

'Is it possible,' says Faller, 'that you were scared? That John could've done something that didn't fit into your life? Is it possible that you already knew he might be a danger?'

'Now, you listen here!' Zandvoort's stood up from his chair. 'Don't try to pin anything on me.'

'Sit down, sir,' says Calabretta.

'I'd like to call my lawyer,' says Zandvoort, sitting down. It sounds like resignation.

'Our colleagues in Aachen,' Faller says, 'have told us about a girl who fits John's pattern.'

'I'm not saying another word,' says Zandvoort. 'Forget it.'

Mr Borger leans back with a smile.

'Very good,' he says. 'It won't be long before we have everything we want to know.'

'What do you think?' I ask. 'Does he have anything to do with Basso's murder too?'

'I can't say,' he says. 'But he's under serious pressure.'

BY MISTAKE

Heiner Matzen seems calm. He's sitting on a chair in the dark room behind the mirrored glass. Ali is with him. The big man stands beside him the whole time, his hand on his shoulder. I'm sitting next to Heiner, Faller's standing right next to the window. We've built a kind of human bunker.

'There is no way that they can either see or hear you,' I say, 'OK?'

'OK,' says Heiner.

The door to the room on the other side opens and Brückner leads in a group of men with bomber jackets, jump boots and shaved heads, Lechner is there too. Two of the guys must be the Russians and the rest are presumably from our ranks. They are all holding signs with numbers on them. Heiner doesn't say a word but looks at each of them very carefully.

'And?' I ask.

'I don't know,' he says. 'Give me a minute, I have to remember.'

He looks at Ali for a moment. Ali nods and Heiner takes a deep breath.

'Number two,' he says, 'and number three.'

'Are you sure?' asks Faller.

'Yes,' says Heiner, 'I'm sure. They were both there.'

'Thank you,' I say, 'you can go.'

Heiner Matzen and Ali leave, Faller presses the loud-speaker button.

'Two and three,' he says.

Lechner and his colleagues leave the room. I follow Faller into the room on the other side of the mirror.

Brückner has already settled down at the table with one of the Russians.

'Where's the other one?' asks Faller.

'Schulle's taken him off next door to look after,' says Brückner.

The man sits on his chair, legs spread, his hands on his thighs. It's the same choreography as with Zandvoort just now, except that it's now Brückner sitting at the interview table instead of Calabretta. Faller is standing by the wall, I'm lurking unobtrusively near the door.

'Where were you last Wednesday evening between nine and half past ten?' asks Brückner.

Silence.

'We think you beat a man to death,' says Brückner.

Nothing.

'Listen, the man fought back. We found skin particles under his fingernails, and I bet they belong to you and your colleague,' says Brückner. 'All we have to do is compare them and you're for it.'

The guy looks him in the eyes.

'You'd do better to open your mouth,' says Brückner. 'Comes over well in court.'

The guy leans forward, his face comes menacingly close to Brückner's. I can see Faller tense his muscles.

'He wasn't meant to die.'

'But he did die,' says Faller.

The guy turns to him. 'By mistake. We only beat him a bit.'

'Why did you beat him?' asks Brückner.

'Money,' says the guy, shrugging his shoulders, 'good money.'

'How much money?' asks Faller.

'Twenty thousand.'

That's a lot for one punch in the gob. Poor Basso, he really did know something.

'Who?' asks Brückner.

The guy looks blankly at him.

'Who paid you?'

'Don't know him,' says the guy, 'he had hood on, didn't see his face.'

Faller calls his men in. He has the guy taken away and the other one fetched. Fresh start, new beginning, same palaver. Things go pretty much the same with the second guy as with the first. Except that this one is even quicker to plead manslaughter than the bloke who was sitting at the table just now. But as for who hired them: zip.

Faller actually believes them. He says these boys have no reason to protect their client. They'll have been paid, they'll have put the money away, and they know they'll do time. When they get out, there'll be a heap of dough waiting for them somewhere. So why would they owe anyone loyalty?

'I'm going to Carla's,' I say, once we're done with them both. 'I need a drink.'

Faller tilts his head, looks sidelong at me.

'Zandvoort's seriously pissing me off,' I say. 'He needs to come clean, not call his lawyer.'

'OK,' he says. 'I'm driving to Ohlsdorf – it's Margarete Sinkewicz's funeral in an hour. Let's see if Iron Siggi turns up.'

We smile at each other. Then we each go our own way.

RELAX, RILEY

It's pretty quiet at Carla's. Only two tables are in use, Belle and Sebastian are singing from the speakers over the counter, under them stands Scott, who's reading the sport section. Carla's not there.

'*Awright, doll*', he says.

Don't call me doll.

'Hey,' I say, 'where's Carla?'

'*She's gone to the market*,' he says.

'Can I have a coffee?' I ask.

'*Sure, doll.*'

Man, Scott.

I sit at a table by the window, Scott comes over with the coffee, bringing the sport section over with him, and puts it down for me.

'Thanks,' I say.

'*My pleasure*,' he says.

An hour, a sport section and two cups of coffee later, I feel a little better and I'm about to leave when Zandvoort walks through the door. He sits down at my table and looks me in the eyes. I run cold.

'So,' he says, 'how was I?'

'Excuse me?'

'You know exactly what I mean,' he says. 'Don't tell me nobody was watching me from behind the mirrored glass. I bet you were there too.'

I don't answer.

He turns to Scott and orders a water, then he leans back and looks out of the window.

'Now your case is closed,' he says, 'we can start again from the beginning.'

Excuse me? Are you nuts?

'You seemed a little tense the other day,' he says. 'But I presume that's eased now. So, shall we have dinner this evening?'

He must be mad.

'My case isn't closed yet,' I say. 'We still have a murder to clear up.'

'Aha,' he says. 'So my dead son is still slashing whores?'

'Exactly which hell did you spring from, Zandvoort?'

Scott brings him his water, Zandvoort grins.

'Just relax a little, Riley.'

'I promise you,' I say, leaning over the table to him, 'that I will only relax once I've found out everything about you, I want to see everything, down to the very last grain of dirt. You attracted me, and even if I have no idea why you decided to play this little game with me, now you'll get it in the neck. And I'm fucking tenacious. I'll pin anything I can on you. I'll make you suffer.'

'Wow, you're crazy,' he says.

He knocks back his water and once he's drunk it, there's a crack, the glass shatters in his hand. He drops the broken glass, stands up and leaves.

FC ST PAULI MADE ME THIS WAY

The pink sky from this morning has transformed into a deep grey, and as I cross the Heiligengeistfeld, it starts drizzling. I'm getting cold. The Millerntorstadion is in front of me, beyond it there's the left turn into my road, I'm almost home, I pull my coat tighter around my body but it isn't enough.

Maybe it's time for a thick football jumper. I'm not really the fan-clothing type, I don't even own a scarf, but I'm thirty-eight, I don't have much time left to change anything, I'll be getting set in my ways soon. I'm ever going to do it, it has to be now. The season's in its closing phases. The team is getting down to business. There's a winning streak in the air. You have to believe in this kind of shit sometimes.

I hold course for the Sankt Pauli Fanshop, a low-slung collection of containers covered with dirty graffiti, the heavy metal door is shut, I have to pull hard to get it open. Inside, behind the counter, are young people with dyed-black hair and stoned eyes, the shelves and rails are crammed with anything you can print *FC St Pauli* on. I run my finger over the things, over T-shirts and scarves and caps in black, brown, white and sometimes even in pink, but I find pink silly. At the back, in the men's section, there's a large, brown hoodie next to the mirror, which has a large, white death's head printed on the chest.

I take it off the hanger and touch it.

Hard on the outside, soft on the inside.

I take off my coat, hang it on a clothes rail and pull the sweatshirt over my roll-neck. The woman in the mirror is taller than I thought. Her brown, sloppily, brushed hair falls thick and heavy onto her shoulders, her features aren't exactly hard but they are definite, and although there are a few lines around her green eyes, the woman looks almost ageless. Her face isn't particularly German. More American. Her body, on the other hand, is Hamburg. Lean, upright and brown-and-white, oversized jumper. Is that me?

I'm not sure.

OK, what the hell, I go to the cash desk and say: 'Can I keep this on?'

The guy at the till says: 'Yup.'

There's a sign on the wall above his head:

FC St Pauli made me this way.

SEVEN MINUTES

It's just after five. I'm sitting in my dressing gown in my kitchen, painting my toenails. No idea what the point is. Well, yes, Klatsche said: we'll go out somewhere smart for dinner this evening. I have to smile at myself. I've just finished my left foot when there's a knock at the door. Klatsche, I think, in my obvious messed-up state, and walk to the door, open it and freeze. Zandvoort. I'm barefoot and when I'm barefoot, I feel naked. I want to shut the door again but he wedges his foot into it. I take a deep breath and open the door again.

'What are you doing here?' I ask.

'I want to talk to you,' he says.

His dark suit rucks a little, he's wearing a pale overcoat that doesn't suit him at all, somehow, the whole ensemble looks a little scruffy. There are beads of sweat on his upper lip. He doesn't seem as cool as normal.

'OK,' I say, and let him in. The second I've closed the door behind him, I know that this wasn't such a good idea.

He heads straight down the hall to the living room, leans against the windowsill and waits for me there. His expression is dark and he shows no sign of talking. OK, must be my line then.

'Where did you get all the dosh?' I ask.

'What dosh?'

'To fund your fancy flat,' I say, 'to fund the flash car that you barely drive, to fund your nice life. The theatre doesn't pay that well.'

'My wife was loaded,' he says. 'Her money was her best feature.'

'Oh,' I say, 'how charmingly you speak about her.'

'Tch,' he says, spittle spraying, 'she wasn't all there, just like her fine gentleman of a son. And she drank like a fish.'

He keeps his head down and looks up at me, it's like he's lying in wait, his hands are hidden in the coat pockets.

'Was she drunk when the accident happened?' I ask.

'Of course,' he says, 'my old lady was always drunk.'

'What exactly happened back then?'

What the hell am I, his therapist? Shit. I shouldn't be asking him questions, I should be kicking him in the balls.

He lifts his head, shuts his eyes and smiles. When he opens his eyes again and looks at me, his expression is so far away it shocks me. I know that look, I've seen it on other people, and now I understand what's going on: here's a man coked up to his eyeballs. And an epileptic, apparently. That's not good, that's not good at all. He shakes his head and smiles, the beads of sweat on his upper lip tremble.

'What did you actually want to talk to me about?' I ask. 'Either you talk or you leave. Right now.'

His eyes dart up to the ceiling, to the floor and then out of the window.

'That Basso was such a miserable little rat.'

'You know he's dead,' I say.

'Naturally,' he says, and his weird smile tips over into a repulsive grin. 'People talk.'

'Oh really?'

'Oh, you know what people round here are like,' he says, 'they're so very chatty, just can't keep their mouths shut.'

I pull myself together.

'So how come,' I say, 'someone like you, from the fancy cultural scene, knew a guy like that Basso?'

'Everyone knew Basso,' he says disdainfully. 'Mister I'm Collecting Protection Money These Days.'

'Did you pay?' I ask.

'Please,' he says, 'nobody paid. Not him. He was a worm.'

I'm not sure whether or not I should go through with this. I can't decide, so for the time being, I continue.

'Was he blackmailing you?'

'What if he was?'

The look in his eyes could have been carved from ice.

'Would you have paid up?'

'What would anyone have to blackmail me about?' His eyes narrow to tiny slits.

'I'm wondering that too,' I say.

He takes his left hand out of the coat pocket and runs it over his brow and through his hair. His right hand stays put. He messes up his normally so perfect hair, two lank strands flop over and hang down onto his face. Maybe he doesn't have such strong nerves after all. Maybe I can crack him now. And then I'll have him in the palm of my hand.

I straighten up. Fine. Let's step into the ring.

'Let's assume,' I say, 'that Basso had been stupid enough to blackmail you.'

His cheeks droop, his face becomes a grotesque.

'Let's just start by assuming that,' I say.

'Do you think I'd be stupid enough to let myself be black-mailed?'

He can't prise his teeth apart properly now, his jaws look like they've been screwed shut, his words can only just crawl through.

'Probably not,' I say.

'Quite,' he says, 'I wouldn't have put up with that.'

My feet are cold.

'What would you have done then?' I ask.

'I'd have made him understand his place,' he says, 'categori-cally. And the bloody stupidity of trying to put a spoke in the wheel of someone like me.'

My phone rings. Damn. Not now.

Zandvoort's jaw seems to harden further, he rubs his left hand over his chin and looks out of the window. I turn away and answer the phone.

'Hello?' I say.

'It's me.'

Faller.

'Ah,' I say, 'Mr Cash.'

'What?' asks Faller.

'Thanks for calling back,' I say.

'Er, yes,' he says, 'I just wanted to tell you that of course Iron Siggi was indeed at Margarete's funeral, and guess what...'

'Yes,' I say, 'that sounds interesting.'

I hope that Faller will interpret my absurd conversational tactics correctly and get on with asking yes-no questions.

'Chastity,' he says, 'is there something you need to tell me?'

Bingo.

'Yes,' I say, 'that would work well.'

'Are you at Zandvoort's?' he asks.

'No,' I say.

'Is he at yours?'

Faller, you old clever clogs.

'That's right,' I say.

'Is everything OK?' he asks.

'No,' I say.

'Fine,' he says, 'I'll—'

And at that moment, my telephone leaves my ear and there's a gun barrel at the nape of my neck. Wow, where did that spring from? If he pulls the trigger, I'm dead.

'Who was that?'

Zandvoort's voice is thin and toneless. My knees are threatening to give way, and I'm praying that they don't because then I'd have a bullet in my head. I don't answer. The pressure on my neck increases.

'Who was that? Was it one of your cops?'

'No,' I say, blurting out the first thing that comes to mind: 'It was just the dry cleaners.'

I narrow my eyes. There's no way he'll buy that. He breathes.

'Give me the fucking gun,' I say.

'No way,' he says, 'no way.'

He steers me over to the window, the gun pressed into my neck.

'Look at the road,' he says.

I see my road below the window, the place where I feel secure, and it occurs to me that it wouldn't be the worst thing to peg out with a view of this street.

'It's nothing special,' he says.

'That's not true,' I say.

'Shut up,' he says.

My legs start shaking.

'Women,' he says. 'You're all the same, always the same shit. Think you're so special, you and your little worlds.'

Ah. So that's what this is about. Women in general and all that.

'You think you've got everything under control,' he says. 'My wife thought that too, she thought she could do everything by herself. She didn't need me, she said. She wouldn't even let me into her bed anymore. Go and have a shower, she said, go and have a shower and jerk yourself off, but keep your hands off me. It went on that way for six months. D'you know how long half a year can be when you're constantly being humiliated? I wasn't such a bad guy when I married her, but she screwed me up. And then at last that lorry came along and just shaved off her head.'

The pressure of the gun on the back of my neck eases a little.

'That's nothing to do with me,' I say.

'Shut it,' he says. 'Just shut it. You're just the same as her. Strolling through your city, so self-satisfied, thinking you're the boss. And you look so fucking like her. You have no idea how like her you look.'

John. Now I understand. That's why he stared at me like that when he was sitting on the bollard down by the jetties, and I had no clue about anything. Shit, what a stupid coincidence. Zandvoort presses the gun harder again, he presses his body against my back and then he shoves his hand under my dressing gown, fast and hard, and grabs me from behind, between the legs.

'You fucking whore.'

He grips harder. It hurts. There it is again, and this time it's unequivocal: I'm the prey and he has the power.

'Can you feel anything?'

I can't speak, I can hardly breathe, my vision slides.

'You know,' he says, 'I can't feel anything down there anymore. The meds I have to take since this disease broke out, just because my idiot wife couldn't control her car and they said I'd suffered a shock, fucking doctors, what do they know about what those shitting pills do to a man, those fucking pills, they fuck everything up, they leave you just a fucked-up piece of meat. It won't work anymore, nothing works anymore. It just doesn't function.'

His mouth is by my ear, the muzzle of the pistol is in my nape like a vice.

'I only wanted the little bitch to dance for me,' he says, 'that stupid cow. All she had to do was prance around a bit. Basso got her for me, but she was such a bitch, wanted more, I could see it in her, she goaded me.'

His hand between my legs grips even harder.

'And then I fucked her, she wanted it that way, she wanted a proper seeing-to for once, but it didn't work because she wouldn't help me out, such a slut, she actually fought back, how are you meant to get it up if they lead you on then turn you down. And then she ran off screaming, and John, the utter moron, saw her and ran after her and then he did the thing he was talking about doing that evening when he was bawling his eyes out in Aachen, the cretin. I went to the effort of getting him out of there when they found that girl. And then, on the evening the little slut was at our place, Basso saw John with her, and two days later, when the newspapers were full of two dead dancers – ha-ha, dancers, as if – he turned up in front of me and kicked up a stink, he wanted to screw me over. Are you scared, you slag?'

'Yes,' I say. 'I am. Stop it, Zandvoort. Take the gun away and stop it.'

'The gun, ha-ha, you changed once that was gone.'

My gun? Is that my own gun pressed into my neck? It's insane, but something rebels inside me. Nobody touches my gun, nobody but me.

'Put the gun down, Zandvoort,' I say, 'right now.'

He laughs. It almost shakes him a little, and his grip loosens slightly, but not enough.

'What did you do to Basso?' I ask, no idea where I'm finding the guts.

'I sent the Russians round, like I did to you,' he says. 'And now shut up.'

He's breathing into my ear and moving his hand back and forth between my legs. I can't hold out much longer, my legs won't hold me long, my brain is whirling, I'm thinking about Klatsche, I'm thinking about Carla, I'm thinking about God, not that I know the hell why, but yeah, help me, I think, please, someone has to help me now, and then there's a massive thud and the door flies open.

'Drop the gun, Zandvoort.'

Faller. He's here.

Zandvoort lets go of me and turns around. I fall against the window and try to grab hold of the windowsill, but it doesn't work and then I'm lying down, the room blurs before my eyes and everything that happens next happens in slow motion, but it happens. Two shots. Zandvoort tips longways onto my floor and dark blood starts to flow out of his side. He's still holding my pistol in his hand.

'Chas,' says Faller, 'are you OK?'

It's only now that I see him turning pale. And then I see the hole under his left shoulder.

'Faller,' I say.

'I'm all right,' he says. 'You take the gun off him.'

'I can't,' I say.

'You can,' says Faller. 'Come on, do it.'

I do it, while Faller crumples in the doorway. I take the gun from Zandvoort while Faller grows ever paler. I crawl over to him while he starts shivering.

'Faller,' I say.

''S OK,' he says.

'Hold on, Faller,' I say, and then I've finally got my hands on my stupid phone. Faller looks at me.

'Chas...' he says, 'I...'

'Shhh,' I say, calling an ambulance.

Seven minutes, they say.

'Two minutes, Faller,' I say, 'two minutes.'

He tries to keep his eyes open, but can't manage it. And he wants to tell me something. I slide closer to him, sit beside him, hold him. There's blood trickling from the corner of his mouth, I try to pretend there's nothing wrong, Faller doesn't like a big drama.

'Iron,' he says.

'Siggi? What about him?'

'Maggie,' he says.

'Yes,' I say. 'What about Maggie?'

He exhales, shuts his eyes.

'OK, Faller,' I say, 'OK.'

IT DOESN'T LOOK GOOD

Two men and a woman: two paramedics and a doctor. They've got equipment with them and they're doing what they can. I'm sitting a few metres away and holding on to the floor with my hands. My feet are so cold that they might have dropped off.

The men lift Faller onto a stretcher and are in the process of carrying him out. The woman asks me if I'm worried.

I nod.

'Your colleagues are on their way,' she says.

I nod again.

'We're taking him to hospital, to Altona,' she says.

'How is he?' I ask.

She doesn't reply.

Thanks to:

Karen Sullivan and everyone at Orenda Books
Rachel Ward
Werner Löcher-Lawrence
Thomas Halupczok
Steve Calabretta
Marcel Eger
Johnny Cash
my family